MW01139046

The Klass

Part One: Tyros

Dan Klasing

Best wishes!

Dan

7/19/2016

The characters and events portrayed in this book are fictitious. Any similarity to real persons, living or dead, is coincidental and not intended by the author.

Published by *Orb of Time Books, LLC*

This is a book of fiction. Any description of scientific discoveries or other technologies is purely coincidental.

Again, this is a work of fiction.

LEARN MORE ABOUT THE KLASS SERIES BY
LIKING: www.facebook.com/TheKlassBooks/

Tyro – [tahy-ro](noun), plural tyros. A beginner, trainee, neophyte, or student.

In its original Latin, a recruit.

Prelude

Article II, Section 3 of the United States Constitution requires the President to inform the Congress from "time to time" of the "state of the union." Most believe this means the President must report on the country's economic condition, military status, and foreign policy initiatives, but they're wrong. In fact, the drafters of the Constitution didn't know if their patchwork of states, held together by the fragile stitches of multiple compromises, would or could remain one country at all. The very existence of the "United States of America" depends first and foremost on whether the states are "united," or have a "union," or not. The framers embodied the critical nature of the relationship between the various states in a Constitutional requirement for the President to gauge, and report on, the state of their union.

The union between the states that make up the world's largest economy and most powerful military has always been far more fragile than appearances would have one believe. Despite the wishes of its first president, George Washington, political parties began to appear before the first year of his first term came to an end. The Federalists, led by Alexander Hamilton with the Northern states of New England as constituents, believed in a strong central government supported by a standing national army. The Democratic-Republicans, led by Thomas Jefferson and supported by the slave-holding agricultural South, insisted that the Federalists desired a return to monarchy and immediate abolition of slavery. Anger and mistrust pervaded the relationship between the founding fathers and between the original thirteen states. The brand-new country's union of states could not have been more tenuous. In fact, both Hamilton and Jefferson persuaded Washington to serve a second term in order to preserve the union itself. Thomas Jefferson is credited with saying that the North and South would hang together only if they had Washington to hang on to.

For the next seventy years, the differences between North and South continued to pull at the bonds that held the states together. The unrelenting economic, moral, and political stresses between the Northern states and the South finally led to open civil war. The North called this the War of Rebellion, while the Southerners referred to it as the Second American Revolution or The War Against Northern Aggression. Whatever its name, the South went to war only after severing its ties to the other states, seceding from the union. Popular history insists President Lincoln "saved" the union between the states, but it's more accurate to say that he forced a continued marriage between North and South upon southerners, who desperately wanted a divorce.

After the war, the North dictated the South's future, enforced by the power of the federal government. Ever since, Southerners have believed their values, morality, traditions, and laws have been subjected to unfair and ever-present federal scrutiny. Many

The Klass -Tyros

Southerners resent that Social Security, Medicare, segregation, voting rights, civil rights, gun registration, universal healthcare, and same-sex marriage have been, in their opinion, shoved down their throats. Meanwhile, they recoil at government's merciless taxes on working citizens, while handing out their hard-earned money to those too lazy to work. In order to be heard at all, the South shouts its protest by standing together in every national election.

The genuine state of the union is not strong. The threads holding the union together are weaker than ever. Can they hold? Or will the fabric of the union finally be ripped apart?

ONE

August – Present Day

Michael King carefully lifted the turn signal on his 1971 Mustang and held it there. Old cars have certain idiosyncrasies, and on his, the signal wouldn't stay on by itself. Michael turned off University Boulevard and into the parking lot of his Eta Mu (HM) fraternity house. It was early August at The University of Alabama and he was back for the first time since finishing his freshman year. The convertible's top was down and the car was crammed with badly packed clothes, school supplies, and all the other stuff he needed to outfit his room for the year.

Michael relished the freedom of college life and his entire being felt lighter just arriving back in Tuscaloosa. His parents were great, but often stayed in his business more than he preferred.

Michael wheeled into the lot just a little faster than absolutely necessary. The power steering made it easy to turn the car into a parking spot near the door using only one hand. Plus, he hoped a brother or two would see him. His frat brothers liked his car. Most of them drove new BMWs, Mercedes, or Range Rovers, provided by their parents. Michael was good with a wrench and could work on his own ride and this intrigued his fraternity brothers.

While they often sought out Michael's help with dead batteries or flat tires, he didn't mind. Southern boys respect only a few activities. Hunting, team sports, and golf are about it. But a guy who works on cars passes muster.

Michael grew up in one of the middle-class neighborhoods south of downtown Birmingham. His father, Allen King, worked for an insurance company as the manager of its claims department. Allen's job was stressful, and often thankless. But it was a good job, and he earned every cent of his salary, always doing more than was asked of him. Michael had watched his father go to work each day and come home each night to his family. This consistency impressed on Michael the value of integrity, the force of will to honor his commitments.

Michael and Allen often spent time together on weekends restoring old muscle cars in their garage. Allen was no expert mechanic, but he enjoyed investigating problems and repairing or replacing parts as necessary. Working alongside his son, they had restored several old cars to nice drivable condition—the Mustang was their most recent project.

Michael turned off the 351 cubic inch V-8 and very carefully opened his door. He had pulled in next to Jim Ewell's 4X4 pickup. Jimbo, as he was called by his friends, was a fifth-year senior and Michael was only a sophomore. Scratching the huge red Ford F-150 extended cab would be inadvisable. Jimbo topped six foot three, weighed in at 230, and was the president of his fraternity.

The Ewell family had been running the Republican Party in Alabama for decades and their influence stoked Jimbo's ego.

Michael had washed this giant truck more than a few times last year as a pledge. Nothing pleased the brothers more than making him or some other poor slob wash Jimbo's truck, and then throwing dirt on it to make a second cleaning necessary. But there would be no more of that for Michael. The pledges this year would get to enjoy such torments. Ever since his initiation, Michael was a brother, and immune from hazing.

Michael reached into the back seat and grabbed a laundry basket full of folded clothes and a big duffle bag stuffed with sheets, towels, pillows, and underwear. He threw the duffle over one shoulder and with the basket under his arm, headed toward the front door. A sidewalk led around to the long, wide front porch.

Originally built back in the sixties, the brick building's exterior reflected the appearance of a plantation mansion and it had changed little since. Six brilliant white Doric columns rose two stories over the front porch. Most of the front side rooms on the third floor had access to the porch's flat roof through dormered windows. Rising three stories, it was the most impressive house on fraternity row.

The Eta Mu house stood at the corner of University Boulevard and Campus Avenue. A vast grass lawn stretched from the front porch to the sidewalk running along University. Branches from several massive live oaks spread over the lawn. From the outside, the house exuded Southern grace and charm.

Once through the double front doors, Michael re-shouldered his duffle and made his way into the "parlor," a large open room opulently furnished with traditional style couches, side-tables and lamps all placed formally around a large inoperative fireplace. Wallpaper depicting an English foxhunt adorned the walls, complete with horses and red-jacketed huntsmen. Michael hardly noticed. The frat brothers never used the parlor, reserving it for the entertainment of alumni and guests on football weekends.

Michael turned right down a short hall, through a heavy metal door, and climbed the stairs to the second floor. Except for the front façade and parlor, the rest of the house was simple, practical, even institutional. The brothers occupied very basic dorm-style rooms on the second and third floors, furnished with metal bunk beds and desks. As with college students everywhere, most of the brothers chose to creatively arrange the sparse furniture to take advantage of the cramped space. Michael's room was at the far end of the hall in the back of the house. A bit breathless from his journey from the car, Michael pushed down the handle with his foot and kicked open the door.

"Shit, dude! What the fuck!" shouted Michael's roommate Jackson. "Give me a break!"

Michael glanced a blanket being thrown over the lower bunk. It was obvious from Jackson's positioning, butt up and face down, and the glimpse of two naked legs, toes up, that Jackson was wasting no time following his college major—chasing skirt.

"Jesus, man, how about leaving me a clue next time?" Michael said as he dropped the basket and duffle on the floor and backed out of the room. Shaking his head at Jackson's unusual talent at getting laid, Michael made his way back downstairs, through the dining room, and into the kitchen, hoping there would be something left over from lunch.

"Hey, Carl," Michael said when he saw the frat's long-time head staffer. "Any sandwiches around here?"

"You know there is, Mr. King. Nice to have you back."

"Good to be back. Summer treat you OK?"

"Oh sure. Missus still mean as hell. But I got the last of the kids out of the house. She's goin' up to A&M this year."

Carl was somewhere between fifty and sixty-five, thin, and, like all the other staff, African-American. He wore a white service coat, black pants, and a smile (at least whenever the "brothers" were around). When the brothers noticed him at all, they tended to like Carl. He took good care of the house and minded his own business.

For his part, Carl was OK with this job. He made more money than he could at Tuscaloosa Country Club, and as long as the house stayed clean and the food was provided on time, most of the little assholes didn't even know if he was there or not. Carl couldn't understand

9

parents who paid for their sons to live in such a nice house, all meals provided. Carl considered most of the boys, as he thought of them, to be nothing but white rednecks with money. But he thought a few were all right, one of whom was Michael.

"Thanks, man," Michael said as he grabbed a chicken salad sandwich out of one of the commercial-size refrigerators. "I'm starving."

"How about some lemonade?" Carl said. "It's from that powder, but it's cold as can be."

"Oh yeah, that's awesome," Michael said after he took several big swallows. "It just had to be hotter than hell on moving day."

"Uh huh," Carl grunted. "Gonna get a lot hotter before it cools down."

Michael slid onto a stool next to one of the stainless steel prep tables and attacked the sandwich. After finishing, he placed his glass and plate in the deep wash sink and, after thanking Carl once again, went out the side door and back around to the side parking lot to his car. Opening the trunk, Michael grabbed another load of college gear. As he came up from under the trunk lid, boxes in hand, someone kicked him in the rear.

"Hey, King, that old POS you drive still actually runnin'?"

The kick had been just beyond playful, and caused Michael to lose his grip on the box of assorted notebooks, pens, lamp, and stuff he needed for his desk.

"Jimbo, go find a fat cowgirl that likes oversized trucks and make a calf for your farm," Michael said after straightening up.

"I believe I'll do just that—after I squash your fag-vertible on the way out!" Jimbo scoffed.

"OK, OK Jimbo, don't get your huge panties all in a wad," said Michael, putting two hands up in mock surrender. It wasn't any use playing with Jimbo too much. He was as strong as he was dimwitted. It was best just to let him win.

"Aw, I'm just screwin' around King! I wouldn't risk scratching this badass on your piece of American history anyway," Jimbo said as he climbed up into the cab of the big Ford. Laughing at his own joke, which wasn't too bad really, at least for Jimbo, he backed out and gunned the truck through the parking lot. The noise from the truck's four-inch exhaust pipes could be heard long after the truck had disappeared down University Boulevard.

What a dick, Michael thought as he headed back into the house with his next load. He hoped his roommate would lose his latest conquest quickly and let him finish moving in.

TWO

After leaving the house, Jimbo hurled his truck east on University Boulevard. He was late. And the committee didn't tolerate irresponsibility.

University runs east to west from downtown Tuscaloosa and straight through the campus. Jimbo wove through the campus traffic, passed Druid City Hospital and crossed over McFarland Boulevard. He made his way past several residential neighborhoods and the new Alabama State Mental Hospital, which always made him smirk a little. He continued past quiet Tuscaloosa neighborhoods, which eventually gave way to dilapidated strip malls occupied by payday loan stores and pawnshops. This part of the Tuscaloosa area hadn't changed much in the past fifty years.

Jimbo's destination was the Moonlight Inn, an old but well-kept, two-story motel about 5 miles west of campus. The Moonlight was a Tuscaloosa landmark of sorts; still attracting football fans that booked rooms a year in advance. Seasoned Alabama fans considered it tradition to stay at the Moonlight, at least once, for a game. The rest of the year The Moonlight traditionally hosted illicit weekday liaisons.

Jimbo wheeled his truck into the back parking lot with only minutes to spare. This meeting required privacy and the Moonlight obliged. The attendees had been told repeatedly not to park in front and the motel's owner made sure that no rooms whatsoever were booked in the back on days the committee was there. The rooms on the backside overlooked only undeveloped dense woods.

Jimbo parked next to a black Toyota SUV, opened the door, and hopped down from the cab. He jogged across the parking lot and up a flight of concrete steps to room 222. After knocking exactly four times, the door cracked open and he was admitted. The door closed quickly behind him.

Instead of two shabby beds and a small bathroom, rooms 222 and 224 had been joined into one large conference room. A twelve-foot polished conference table stood on a deep crimson carpet surrounded by high-back black leather chairs. Twelve other people were in the room, all male and most had a drink of some kind in their hand. Jimbo crossed to a granite-topped bar, installed in place of one bathroom, and helped himself to a longneck Budweiser.

"Jimbo! Thought you were going to be late. You're the last one here."

"No way," Jimbo said. "I haven't been late yet and I don't plan on startin' now. So what's on the agenda Bobby?" Bobby represented Tau Tau Omega fraternity. In fact, every man in the room represented a different frat. Each was carefully handpicked by their predecessor to attend these meetings as a member of the controlling committee of an organization called The Tyros.

At least once a month, twelve representatives from the best fraternities at The University of Alabama secretly gathered at The Moonlight Inn to decide on the path The Tyros would follow. The Tyros was supposed to be secret, but it had long ago become the worst kept secret on the Alabama campus. A political organization comprised of the best fraternities and sororities on campus, The Tyros appointed candidates to run for Student Government Association positions and then block-voted them into office. "Independents"—those with no Greek affiliation—rarely won substantial positions.

After being recruited into this secret committee, the members were informed that The Tyros was actually part of a larger organization run by a group called "The Doyens." Extremely powerful and influential alumni, The Doyens pledged to vault these chosen young men into important and lucrative political, business, and professional positions. Once selected, the committee members could count on strong support for the rest of their lives, as long as their commitment to The Doyens remained unfaltering. The Tyros wielded influence not only at Alabama, but could be found at most major Southern universities, if one looked hard enough.

"Same thing that's always on the agenda this time of year: SGA elections," Bobby answered.

"Yeah, I sort of figured," Jimbo said. "What's the big deal? We always win the elections."

"Yeah, but we got problems this year," Bobby explained. "There's a Catholic chick running against The Tyros as an independent. For president! I hear she's too ugly to get herself into any sorority, but she's been picking up a lot of support. You know the deal, The Tyros has to own the presidency, or the rest isn't worth a damn."

"Yeah, I know," Jimbo replied. "What I don't get is how she got so popular in the first place. Your average dumb ass independent out there is like most people everywhere. As long as it doesn't really affect their lives, they don't give a crap what happens in the government. By runnin' the Student Government Association we control housing, intramural sports, student recreation, and a lot of other stuff. Plus we control the money."

"Yep, the student activities fee we all pay every year is a pile of money," Bobby said taking a long pull on his beer. "I gotta think that a independent president of the SGA isn't going to be as generous with those funds to the frats as we are!"

"On top of that, as president she could make trouble for The Tyros in a big way. Naw, it just can't go down like that," Jimbo declared. "Holy crap! I didn't think there was Catholics in Alabama anyway. The Doyens worried about this?"

"They're worried all right," Bobby said confidently. "There's been a lot of moaning around campus about how The Tyros supposedly manipulates the elections every year. Now those liberals over at the newspaper have joined in. Everybody thinks that if we lose this election, the blacks, Asians, and independents will take over, maybe permanently. Hell, we might even lose our seats at the games."

"I suppose our benefactors won't be too thrilled if that goes down," Jimbo observed, suddenly concerned about what The Doyens might do—or refuse to do. "I, for one, would like to keep them happy. My time here's almost up and I'll be counting on their help real soon."

"It's not just here," Bobby explained. "I've heard there's problems at Texas, Mississippi, Georgia, and South Carolina. Hell, even Auburn."

"That's right," Jimbo heard from over his right shoulder. "The Doyens want this stopped and put in reverse. They don't want blacks, hippies, Jews, Catholics, or anyone else taking over our universities. Losing could signal widespread change in attitudes and opinions and even worse, encourage future opposition."

"You got that right Hunter," Bobby agreed.

"OK, enough talk, we're gonna do something about it starting right now," Hunter Dodson declared. In a loud and commanding voice he added, "Let's get started!"

Hunter Dodson III was a senior, blond, and deadly serious. The Doyens controlled The Tyros through this committee. And Dodson controlled the committee. The Doyens, upon the recommendation of the last Chairman, approached and appointed Dodson at the end of last year as the leader of the committee. Dodson was both ruthless and loyal, the very qualities The Doyens required. The Doyens also entrusted him with deeper insight into the larger organization, along with other valuable incentives, and expected results in return.

The rest of the committee's members came from old influential families that had supported "traditional Southern values" for many decades. But, like anywhere else, wealth played the most important role in the member selection process. After all, the more one has, the more one has to lose. The Doyens protected the future of their organization and their class by recruiting and training future generations to be fiercely protective of their status and influence over others.

Hunter stood at the head of the table and called the meeting to order. "OK gentlemen, let's get started!" The room grew quiet as the members moved quickly to their seats. Deciding not to sit himself, Hunter instead leaned over and placed his hands flat on the table, showing he was both deadly serious and in charge.

"OK, we have to do something and we have to do it now. I'm getting heat from above on this one. You know the problem. The Tyros' opponent for president is popular. Too popular. And she has a better than even shot at beating us for the first time in decades. This looks bad for everyone at this table. We are not going to fail! Not on my watch. We need a solution. What are we going to do about this?"

For the next five minutes, representatives floated various ideas. Suggestions ranged from spending more on The Tyros' advertising budget to slandering the opposition candidate on social media. Hunter listened to the discussion, but quickly became irritated by his committee's lack of imagination. The committee members proposed only safe and conventional remedies to a problem that required altogether new thinking.

This election would determine whether the independent student body, those with no loyalty to an organization, and particularly those opposed to The Tyros, could successfully assert control over the SGA. Hunter's success as the committee's Chairman and his very future with The Doyens depended upon The Tyros defeating this one girl. *Conventional means won't work this time; the opposition is too close to victory. No, we need something more than conventional. We need something nuclear!*

"No, no, no," Hunter barked. "We can't out campaign this girl, even with what some might call 'dirty' politics. We just don't have time to convince five or ten thousand idiots not to vote for her, and they'd just see right through anything we do to discredit her. So, if we can't beat her, we have to remove her, uh, convince her to get out of the race."

The room fell silent. Hunter's solution was simple but elegant, and it took committee's members a few seconds to catch up.

"How are we supposed to do that?" Jimbo asked, grinning from the other end of the table. "She ain't going to quit just because we ask her real nice." This made a few of the other members chuckle.

"Then we don't ask real nice," Hunter responded seriously. "Yeah, I think we should have a serious face-to-face talk with her real quick. And in private. We need to … uh … un-gently dissuade her from taking us on. Leave her no choice."

Looking around the room, Hunter saw looks of concern and even some fear. Only Jimbo seemed eager to hear more.

"Jimbo, can you handle this?" Hunter knew Jimbo would jump at the chance to impress him and The Doyens. Jimbo also had fewer scruples than anyone else in the room.

"Hell, yeah. I'll take care of this up close and personal like. You just leave it to me," Jimbo said enthusiastically.

"No," Hunter ordered. "Use The Boys."

Jimbo hesitated. "OK," he finally said slowly. "But you know they get carried away pretty easy." Everyone in the room knew that was an understatement.

"It's your job to make sure they don't. Keep them in line, be sure you can't be tied to anything, and get this done. Now. We're out of time," Hunter ordered.

THREE

Michael gave up the room to his roommate for the rest of the afternoon. He didn't want another close encounter of the naked kind. He used the time to take care of some things at the registrar's office, like paying his tuition. Michael's family helped him with college expenses, but they expected Michael to pay about half of what it cost to attend college each year. He also had to pay his fraternity dues, mostly because his parents didn't believe fraternity membership was a necessary part of his education. They didn't object to him being a member, but Michael had a younger brother who would start college soon, and unlike many other members of the fraternity, his family struggled with the extra expense of college. So he worked hard during the school year to save for college and to pay for dates, gasoline, and anything else he wanted.

During high school, Michael had never considered joining a fraternity. He had heard fraternities were expensive and he was going to have to save a considerable amount of money just to go to college at all. When Michael finally decided to attend The University, his best friend in high school, Zachary Self, talked him into Greek life. Zach convinced Michael that if he were going to have any social life at all, he would need to join a frat. And Zach badly wanted Michael to join Eta Mu with him as a pledge brother. So, Michael saved diligently all summer and committed to several student loans. As it turned out, Zach was right. Michael embraced life in the fraternity and all its social and party opportunities. You only get to be young and in college once.

Zach was popular in high school and made friends easier than anyone Michael ever met. He was perfectly comfortable drinking beer with the jocks, smoking pot with the rockers, or talking about computer games with the nerds. Consequently, he easily won the election for president of their senior class. Considering his charisma, substantial ambition, and need for recognition, Zach's choice to study political science didn't surprise anyone. He wanted to attend law school after graduation, which was generally considered the quickest route to a career in politics. Fortunately, the university had an excellent one right down the road.

Even if his family hadn't been wealthy and living "behind the gates" in one of Birmingham's most expensive neighborhoods, Zach always knew he could get into Eta because of his status as a legacy. Since his father was a past member, Zach was all but assured to be pledged at the beginning of his freshman year.

Michael's chances weren't nearly as good. His family had neither influence nor money and he wasn't a legacy. His family would be considered upper middle class, at best. In the end, Eta pledged Michael because several active members knew and liked Michael from high school and thought he would fit in well. Michael wasn't the poorest member of Eta and a few other members also struggled to pay the fraternity's dues. So far, Michael considered the extra expense money well spent.

Just as Michael reached the bottom steps outside the administration building, his phone rang. It was Zach.

"Hey, I saw your ride in the lot. Are you in the house?"

"No, I had to give the room up to Jackson for a while. I walked down to campus, but I'm on my way back," Michael answered.

"Some of us are heading over to Gallet's to play pool. Why don't you come over?" Zach suggested.

"Sure, why not. I'll see y'all in a minute," Michael agreed. Michael didn't often splurge on bar tabs. But, this was the beginning of the school year and he had more money today than he would have for the rest of the semester.

Michael walked back down University Boulevard toward the frat house. Gallet's was nestled next to a package store directly across the street from the frat house. One of the numerous dive bars lining University Boulevard, Gallet's offered beer, mixed drinks, pool tables, and three shabby booths.

Gallet's hadn't changed in decades. It was always dark inside due to a complete lack of windows and smelled strongly of spilled beer and cigarettes, with a background note of urine and vomit. But Michael wouldn't have it any other way. Over the past year, Gallet's had become a second home. His frat brothers hung out there and it wasn't usually crowded during the week. On weekends, though, it was packed. And on game days, both fans and students overran Gallet's and every other bar on the strip. But this afternoon, the bar was all but empty.

Michael found Zach in the back where several well-worn pool tables stood under three identical lamps, each emblazoned with "Budweiser King of Beers". The tables were old, but played straight. A game cost seventy-five cents. When the tables were busy, you stacked three quarters near the coin slot and waited for the game ahead of you to end. Sometimes there were five or six stacks of quarters lined up. But today, Zach and two other brothers had the tables to themselves. Michael warmly greeted all three with the secret HM handshake.

"Man, it's great to see y'all," Michael said. "What the hell you been up to all summer?"

"Oh man, the usual," Jonathan "Bubba" Adcock said. "My daddy had me working three days a week on the dock unloading trucks. He said I ought to do something to earn my keep. Hard-ass old son of a bitch." Nobody in the world could physically embody the nickname "Bubba" better than Bubba. Standing well over six feet tall with broad, thick shoulders and an impressive beer belly, Bubba left a lasting impression wherever he went—or sat. Bubba's down-home country humor and larger than life personality couldn't be suppressed. Far more intelligent than he let on, most of his good ol' boy persona was just an act. Now a junior, Bubba ranked first in his class in aerospace engineering, maintaining a perfect 4.0 grade point average.

"Three whole days a week!" Michael quipped, slapping Bubba on the back. "You must be just exhausted."

"I outta bring you down there n' make you work on them docks during the summer. Those boys down there all smell like they only take one shower a month and call me 'redneck college boy.' Ain't no air conditioner on the docks either. But I figure, what the hell, it keeps Daddy happy enough to send me back here, so I don't mind so much," Bubba said. "What did you do all summer? Sell ladies shoes in the mall again?"

"That I did, Bubba. And it was cool and smelled like perfume all day long," Michael said laughing.

Zach and the other brother, Stanley Northington, had been watching this exchange, leaning on their pool cues and laughing. Michael and Bubba couldn't have been more different. Michael was from the suburbs while Bubba was from the very small town of Greenville, thirty miles South of Montgomery. Bubba's family owned a string of grocery stores and was quite comfortable. In fact, they were the richest family in at least five counties. Unlike Bubba, no trust fund waited patiently for Michael to turn twenty-one. But outside of his friendship with Zach, Bubba was his closest friend in the house.

Bubba was an excellent pool player despite his immense size. At home in Greenville, Bubba spent an inordinate amount of time playing on his family's professional Olhausen table, so he rarely lost.

"Come on, grab a cue, if you can find one that's halfway straight, and we'll take these two losers on," Zach said to Michael with feigned bravado. "Jimbo said he wanted to see me before dinner for some reason, so I don't have much time."

"What for?" Stanley asked.

"I don't know. Come to think of it, he said not to mention it to anybody, so keep it to yourselves." Zach requested. "He probably wants to put me in charge of making sure the new pledges clean his private john twice a day. Man, I hated that job. But, he's the big man in the house so I guess I better show up."

"I would if I was you," Stanley said. "Jimbo still scares the hell out of me."

"I agree with Stan the Man." Michael chimed in.

"Yep," agreed Zach.

"Well, are we gonna drink beer and play pool or just keep jawing about who's the biggest pussy? By the way Michael, that's you. Your break," Bubba said, vaguely pointing his cue at Michael.

FOUR

It was still light out when Zach jogged across University, over the lawn, and into the frat house.

Dinner was still an hour away, but the house buzzed with brothers moving back in for the year. Zach issued the requisite hellos, but didn't let himself get caught up in conversation. Stopping at the second-floor bathroom, he expelled the two beers he drank at Gallet's. It wouldn't do to interrupt Jimbo just to take a leak. Zach walked up one more flight to the third floor and knocked on Jimbo's door.

"Get your ass in here," he heard Jimbo holler from inside.

Zach opened the door and walked into the biggest residence in the house. Two windows, each set into a dormer, overlooked the front lawn. The room had one double bed, a leather couch placed between the dormer alcoves and a large wooden desk. A new Apple laptop sat squarely on the desk in front of an oversized reclining desk chair. Jimbo sprawled in the corner of the couch, one foot propped on a coffee table in front of him. A bottle of Jack Daniels Black and two glasses rested near his foot.

"Hey Jimbo, what's up?" Zach asked as he entered somewhat tentatively. Zach had never been invited to this room before, except to clean his toilet with a toothbrush.

"Come on in and sit down," Jimbo said, motioning to a lawn chair opposite the couch— the same chair Jimbo used when he wanted to sit on the roof over the front porch. "I need to talk with you about something. Have some of this," Jimbo offered, pouring some Jack Black into one of the glasses.

"Thanks," Zach said, picking up the drink. Zach still had no idea what Jimbo wanted with him, and this fact kept him a little uncomfortable.

"This conversation's private. So don't go runnin' your mouth about it. Got it? I seen you workin' hard on the SGA elections last year. In fact, it looked to me and some others that you were maybe the best campaigner we had, and you was only a freshman," Jimbo began.

"Thanks. The elections are important, but I was just trying to do my part," Zach said, attempting to appear modest.

"Ha!" Jimbo blurted. "You can't bullshit a bullshitter. You knew exactly what you were doing. Making a play to get noticed early. We like that. Shows you want to go places. I'm right, aren't I?"

"OK. Yeah," Zach said, now a little perturbed by Jimbo's probing. "I admit it, I want to run for election at some point. I know I've got to start at the bottom, but that's OK. I just don't want to spend much time in the Little Leagues. Who's "we" anyway?"

"Don't worry about that. Right now all I want to know about is where you stand, and you still aren't tellin' me what I want to know. Spit it out, this is just a friendly chat between friends. Give it to me. What do ya really want?"

Zach took a moment to try and figure out what Jimbo was up to. Why the interrogation? Why the sudden interest in him? Zach took a sip of his drink and let the fiery liquid slip down his throat. At the same time, his ambition rose to the surface. Always on the lookout for an opportunity, Zach decided to go for broke. "I want to be president of the SGA in my senior year and then go to law school. Afterward, I want to go to the House and then be one of the two senators from the State of Alabama." Zach shrugged, but looked Jimbo dead in the eye. "You asked."

"Whoa, ambitious, huh? Good. Seeing as how you've given this a lot of thought, just how do you plan to get elected SGA president?" Jimbo asked with a knowing smile.

Zach took another sip of Jack Daniels, playing for a few seconds to think. His answer had to be the right one. Zach sat back and answered, "Hard work and loyalty to Eta."

"That's a good start. But you didn't mention The Tyros," Jimbo said.

There it is! Crap! He should have known. Zach's father had mentioned being a Tyros candidate when he had been an Eta, but now he knew the perfect answer. "I'm a Tyros guy all the way. My dad worked hard for The Tyros when he was here. I'm going to do everything in my power to make sure The Tyros candidates win every race this year, next year, and the next. Thirty years from now my son or daughter will do the same," Zach said earnestly.

"All right then! Them's some big words, but the right ones," Jimbo commented. "The Tyros has been running this campus for decades and it needs to stay that way. Loyalty to us will take you a long way," Jimbo paused a moment, taking a sip of his own drink.

"There's no doubt in my mind about any of that," Zach said. He liked where this was going.

"Here's the thing," Jimbo went on. "I help choose who runs and for what place." Jimbo held up his glass and slowly swirled the amber liquid around the sides, pausing briefly to emphasize his own importance. "My, uh, committee, needs someone to run for SGA Senate. One of our candidates had to drop out. We need a replacement and that person needs to be an Eta. That Eta is going to be you."

Zach could hardly believe what he was hearing! *He was only a sophomore, but the frat apparently wanted him to run for Senate? This is a dream come true!*

"Are you kidding?" Zach managed to say. "I mean, yeah, sure. Sounds great." Zach tried to act at least a little cool about it, but failed.

"Well, I gotta get you approved and you sure ain't won any election yet, so don't go gettin' a big stiffy. But I think you're just the guy who can win and can take directions. A lot of important stuff rides on these things so we gotta be sure you're the guy."

"Yeah, sure. I get it," Zach replied. "I can handle it."

"OK, look, I'll bring it up. We're getting together soon to make decisions on this stuff. Nothin' is guaranteed, but *I* can make it happen."

"Thanks, man!" Zach said smiling. "I'm your guy." Zach lifted his glass and took a long sip of the bourbon. "Just tell me what to do, and I'll do it."

"Now," Jimbo said finishing his drink, "that's just what I wanted to hear."

FIVE

Drew Campbell boarded his flight and awkwardly shuffled down the aisle of the plane trying not to let his laptop case hit other passengers while rolling his carry-on bag behind him. Drew had flown from Los Angeles to Las Vegas that morning, in order to catch a flight to Birmingham, which was as close as he could get to his home in Tuscaloosa.

Drew hefted his carry-on suitcase into the overhead compartment, took off his suit coat, throwing it on top of his bag, and slid into his seat, 25B. Drew was over six feet two inches tall and vexed, as usual, at how little room there was for his knees in the cheap seats. Drew shoved his laptop case under the seat in front of him by putting one leg into the aisle. He then managed to fish his seatbelt from under his thigh and get it fastened. Finally settled, Drew noticed the male passenger in seat 25A, the window seat, was already asleep.

Drew, a lawyer, had attended the deposition of a truck accident expert in California representing one of his law partner's clients. He usually didn't have to travel much, but he volunteered to take this trip when his partner's father suddenly became ill. *No good deed goes unpunished*, Drew thought, not for the first time on this trip. The deposition forced him to sit in a conference room with eight other lawyers for over ten straight hours yesterday. And LA traffic could only be described as punishment for the damned. Exhausted, he looked forward to doing nothing on the four-hour flight home except read the new novel he bought at the airport.

Drew loosened his tie and made himself as comfortable as possible in the small seat. He didn't like traveling. The pressure to take everything he needed, be at a particular gate at a particular time, obey all security details, and keep track of a boarding pass was just a big hassle as far as he was concerned. Drew preferred a more convenient and ordered existence. He liked to leave work on time, go home and relax at the end of the day with a glass of wine and a good book. Life presented plenty of stress without having to haul his carcass across country to listen to the opinions of some overpaid "expert" on accident reconstruction. Drew's hair was dark brown, but grey was beginning to assert itself more and more. Drew declared to anyone who would listen this was the result of running a law firm all day while trying to actually practice, and then coming home to two teenage girls in the flower of their adolescence.

After taxiing around the airport into takeoff position, the 707 finally climbed into the air. From several thousand feet Drew thought the fabulous Las Vegas strip looked like a strange amusement park someone abandoned in the desert. The acceleration and steep ascent didn't seem to bother Drew's sleeping companion in the seat next to him. Thirty minutes later and two chapters into his novel, the flight attendant came by Drew's seat with the drink cart. Probably not noticing the man next to

Drew was asleep, she asked, "Can I get you something to drink sir?"

The man stirred and asked for a Diet Coke. "I'm glad you're OK," Drew said jokingly. "I was beginning to wonder."

"Sorry," the man said. " I guess I just passed out as soon as I sat down."

"Tough time at the casinos?" Drew said.

"No, this is just the first time I've been able to relax at all in about three months."

"Work?" Drew asked.

"Yeah, I was on a team working on a big government contract. It was rush, rush, rush. They can push hard when there's something new they want very badly."

"Something special?" Drew asked.

"You could say that," responded the tired and somewhat disheveled looking guy. "Part of a defense project."

"Sounds like exciting work," Drew said, now interested enough to continue the conversation.

"It's quite fascinating, really. I developed a new way to align jet turbine blades, which the big military brass seemed to like a lot. Well, I guess it's exciting for me." He obviously didn't want to bother Drew if he didn't want to hear more.

"Can you tell me about it? I'm kind of an aviation voyeur," Drew said. An airplane buff since he was a small boy, Drew still enjoyed learning about military aircraft in particular.

"An aviation voyeur? Ha! That's a good one. Sure. I'm Rick Donnelly, by the way." Rick said as he stuck out his hand.

"Drew Campbell," Drew said taking Rick's hand.

"Nice to meet you, Drew. Anyway, you know how jet engines use turbine blades to compress the air entering and exiting the engine? They're really just big fans." Drew nodded. "Well, it's critical that those fan blades, for best performance, be aligned properly. Before my thing, the blades had to be aligned by hand, one at a time. I just worked out a way that they could be aligned all at once and with more accuracy. I work for Pratt & Whitney."

"Wow! Sounds complex. You must be an engineer?"

"Yeah, engineer, physicist, and glorified airplane mechanic. At the moment, I'm simply an overworked government contract employee," Rick said smiling.

Drew said, "Well that's a lot more interesting than what I do. I'm a lawyer that does work for insurance companies mostly."

"I don't know about that," Rick said. "I really don't know any lawyers or even what you guys do, except what I see on TV."

The two went on chatting for some time. Drew quizzed Rick about his work, eager to learn about a subject totally different than his sometimes-mundane law practice. Drew respected engineers. They actually got to design, build, and improve things. He had even considered studying engineering, but a lackluster interest in mathematics during his youth had been the deal-breaker.

Rick told him that the particular Pratt & Whitney engine he was working on was being used in a new military fighter/bomber. Drew couldn't hide his enthusiasm to hear more. Curiosity overwhelming the little voice in his head cautioning not to pry into the subject much further, Drew asked: "Can you tell me about the plane or is it secret or classified or something?"

"I can tell you it's a military aircraft, the YF-twenty-six," Rick said with some pride. "I can also tell you it's an awesome plane, superior to anything in the air right now. It's a single seat, twin-engine fighter/bomber. The hardest part to designing it was meeting the specifications of the Navy, Air Force, and Marine Corps. It had to be capable of landing on an aircraft carrier for the Navy, providing long-range supersonic interception capability for the Air Force, and handling close air support for the Marines. On top of all that, it had to have the radar cross signature of a small bird."

"How'd you guys manage to put that puzzle together?" Campbell was close to enthralled with this conversation.

"Ah, puzzle is an apt description," Rick began. "The answer is with vectored thrust. That's where the thrust from the engines can be pointed several degrees from directly aft of the plane in any direction. This allows maneuverability in the air like nothing before. Plus, it can land and take off on two hundred feet of roadway if needed. The stealth capabilities are really cool, but I can't talk about that. Anyway, I worked on the engines. Because of limited space, they had to be more powerful, but overall much smaller than previous generations. In other words, they had to be hyper-efficient. That's where I came in. The tooling was really exceptional, it required a special alloy that could bend precisely while in use." Rick stopped suddenly. "Oh man, sorry, I get all worked up talking about this stuff."

"Are you kidding? That's fascinating! Please go on," begged Drew.

Rick saw that his seatmate was actually eager to hear more. "OK, here's a fact you will find interesting. Since the place is no longer a secret, I can tell you we conducted our final development and testing at Groom Lake."

Drew's eyes widened like a six-year-old kid on Christmas morning. "Area 51? Really?" Drew said in a profoundly awed half-whisper.

"Absolutely. I was there for several months, during its testing. I can tell you it ain't no resort; but it's absolute paradise for an aerospace engineer."

Drew was amazed, shocked really. He had, of course, heard about Groom Lake. He had watched several documentaries about the top-secret base and the experimental aircraft developed there over the years. Drew desperately wanted to ask more about Area 51, but he managed to bite his tongue. Drew didn't want to put Rick on the spot and he didn't want to look like some slack-jawed UFO nut.

"Wow," Is all Drew managed to say while trying to come to grips with the coolest thing he ever heard.

Drew desperately wanted to ask Rick more questions, but by this time the two had been talking for a long while and Rick looked tired again. He was slumped against the side of the aircraft with his arms crossed. Drew thought he had fallen asleep. But, through half closed eyes, Rick said, "Yeah, it's probably the most incredible place on earth." Then he asked, looking at Drew with one open eye, "Do you watch *Star Trek*?"

"Sure, I'm a *Next Generation* guy. Don't tell anyone, but I wish I had one of those uniforms. I'd probably get disbarred, divorced, and thrown out of my neighborhood if I actually wore one."

Rick grinned and closed his eyes. "Well," he said, "they have most of that stuff already." And, with that rather mind-blowing revelation, Rick settled deeper in his seat and fell fast asleep.

Drew didn't know what to think. He didn't know if Rick was being serious or not. But, he thought, who could, or would, make up a story about aligning jet compressor blades on Pratt & Whitney engines? Drew was, if anything, reasonable and logical. Since he would never really know for sure, there wasn't any reason to either totally dismiss or believe what Rick said. Drew tried to put Rick's story out his mind, but failed miserably.

About a half an hour before landing at the Birmingham airport, Rick woke again. Drew didn't ask anything else about Area 51. But, as friendly as ever, Rick offered Drew his business card and asked for Drew's in return.

"Since you're interested in aircraft, I'll send you some eight-by-ten glossies of the different airplanes that use our engines. All military." Rick promised. "You can give them to your kids or whatever," he said with a smile.

"Alright! Thanks. But we both know I'm not giving them to my kids." Drew laughed.

"Great," Rick said. "I'll drop some in the mail for you as soon as I get back to my office in Baltimore in a day or two."

When the plane landed, Drew and Rick parted company. Drew found his car and started the hour-long drive home to Tuscaloosa. He didn't think too much more about Rick or Area 51 until a few weeks later. At the moment, he was exhausted and just wanted to get home.

SIX

"Good morning!" Tracy Jenkins said peeking around the door to Drew Campbell's office two weeks after his trip to LA. "Did you have a good weekend?"

Drew looked up from his notepad and peered at the door over the top of his black reading glasses. As usual, Tracy was way too chipper for a Monday morning. Drew, as usual, hid the irritation he felt when Tracy unexpectedly popped into his office. Tracy was Drew's secretary, or "assistant" as she liked to be called. An excellent legal secretary, Tracy was efficient, accurate, and knew how to deal with the Alabama court system. But she just bugged the heck out of Drew.

"Oh, yeah. I hope you did, too." Drew said, thinking his short reply would signal Tracy that he needed to keep reading over his notes. Of course, it didn't work out that way.

Tracy put her hands on the outside of the doorframe and leaned into the office. Tracy was a big girl, and this stance only allowed her stomach to hang farther over her jeans.

"I had a second date with Chuck," she said in her rather sing-song voice. "You remember, the guy I met on Farmersonly.com?" Drew didn't, nor did he care. "Anyway, this came for you I guess on Saturday. Do you want me to open it?" Tracy asked waiving a thick and somewhat dirty manila envelope.

39

Really? Drew thought, she came all the way back to his office to see if she should open an envelope? He had to suppress several very sarcastic remarks that had flown directly to the tip of his tongue.

"Just leave it on my desk. Thanks," Drew was able to answer as he looked back down at his notes. "I'll look at it after Judge Smith gets done denying my motion this morning. I have to look at this and then get down to the courthouse." *Hint, hint, freaking HINT!*

"OK. Don't forget you told Lex you'd go by and renew the boat tag while you were over there today." Tracy said.

"Oh yeah. Thanks, I've been telling her I'd take care of that for a week."

"You're wellllllcommme," Tracy sang as she turned and headed back down the hall.

Drew shook his head and breathed a sigh of relief at her exit. Yet, as much as she put his nerves on edge, he absolutely couldn't get along without her. Over the years he had grown accustomed to that particular paradox in his life.

A few hours later, Drew was back at his desk dictating a letter to his client about how Judge Smith had, indeed, denied his motion. Judge Smith did not like insurance companies, and since insurance companies made up nearly 100 percent of Drew's clients, Judge Smith didn't really like him much either.

Drew finished the letter and dropped the SD card off with Tracy to be transcribed. When he got back into his office, he noticed the thick manila envelope on the edge of his desk where Tracy had left it that morning. It was unusual to get a package like that anymore. Most documents were sent via e-mail. Curious, Drew picked up the package and turned it over. He was a surprised to see that the envelope was from Pratt & Whitney. The company's logo, a flying bald eagle over a green circle embossed with "Pratt & Whitney, Dependable Engines" made it clear this was not related to one of his cases. His name and office address were handwritten and there were numerous stamps in the upper right corner. Then it hit him. The guy from the plane!

"Well I'll be damned," Drew said out loud.

Drew didn't remember Rick Donnelly's name until he opened the envelope and found a stack of pictures and a handwritten note. The note read:

> *Hi Drew. It was a pleasure to talk with you the other day on the plane. Since you are interested in aviation, I thought you would enjoy these shots of the newest fighters. Some haven't entered service yet, but this is the kind of thing I work on. The picture of the aircraft from directly overhead shows how the camouflage paint is supposed to blend with desert environments. The other side is interesting too. If I can, I'll answer any questions you might have about the photos. Thanks!*

The Klass -Tyros

Rick

Drew had forgotten all about Rick's offer to send photographs, but he was more than a little excited to look through them now. He felt like a kid scoring awesome pictures to hang on his bedroom wall.

The photos depicted various aircraft, all fighters or fighter-bombers. The stack of about twenty included glossy 8x10 images of late model fighters using Pratt & Whitney engines, including the new YF-26. The pictures were beautiful, probably used by Pratt & Whitney's promotional department and just the kind of thing an aviation enthusiast would covet. But the last four photos in the stack showed an aircraft Drew didn't recognize at all. *This must be the latest and greatest, he thought*! The craft (Drew hardly recognized it as an airplane) was photographed while on the ground in a hangar and in the air. Drew held two of each.

Puzzled, Drew studied the photos closer. The two pictures of the aircraft in the hangar were both taken from the front. The first was a dramatic wide-angle shot that showed the aircraft was large—perhaps the size of the current B1-B bomber—but didn't provide any detail. The next photo, showing the aircraft in the three-quarter frontal view, revealed a flattened, pointed nose. The rest of the craft's body appeared to flare immediately out from the nose at an extremely shallow angle and wrap back into the fuselage near the back, where a tail or upright stabilizer would normally be. But even looking as closely as possible, Drew couldn't make out an upright tail fin at all.

The third photo was taken in flight, showing the craft from the side. It confirmed that the plane had no upright stabilizer and the tail was no more than a small sharp cone pointing backward. A darkened canopy, really just two windows, occupied the front of a long, low "hump" that started just over the cockpit windows and ran along the top of the fuselage, becoming smaller and smaller as it neared the back of the plane, eventually disappearing altogether near the rear of the craft.

The first three photos puzzled him, but when Drew got to the last picture, he was immediately shocked. "Holy crap," Drew said under his breath. This photo was taken from directly above the plane in flight. The entire thing was shaped almost exactly like a triangle! Only the "tail cone" and a slight change in the angle at the front of each "wing" kept it from actually being perfectly triangular. The odd shape of the plane alone would have left Drew intrigued and profoundly impressed. But it was the presence of two perfectly round openings in each wing that Drew simply couldn't comprehend. The openings were huge, taking up much of what otherwise would be wing surface and the ground was clearly visible through the, well, holes. Taking another look at all four pictures, Drew could find no external engines, intakes, or exhaust nozzles.

Drew looked back at Rick's note. It indicated that the picture of the aircraft taken directly from above would show how the camouflage was suppose to match the desert. Yet, the picture of the triangular craft showed it painted in various shades of very dark greens and black. Desert? That didn't make sense. Then he turned the picture over. In small pencil Rick had written:

> *Drew, I need some advice. I'll be back in Alabama again on 1 October. These are not classified, but please keep the last four pics to yourself and put them somewhere safe; they're not public yet. I'll call you when I get to Alabama.*
> *Many thanks, Rick.*

Confused, but utterly intrigued, Drew put Rick's note and the four photos in his briefcase. The others he left on his desk, thinking maybe he'd frame one or two. He looked at the calendar. October 1 was three weeks away. He decided to just wait and see if Rick actually called.

He did.

SEVEN

After coming into work on the first day of October, Drew checked his calendar. Rick Donnelly was supposed to be in Alabama today. Ever since receiving the pictures and the note from Rick, the question about whether he would actually call and what he might want occupied his mind. *Maybe he was having family issues or needed a will written or something. But, why would he need an Alabama lawyer? And why ask for help on the back of a photo of an advanced aircraft of some kind?*

Drew tried to put his curiosity aside and concentrate on his latest insurance policy brainteaser. As usual, the insurance company wanted to know if a certain building contractor's work was covered by his commercial liability policy. Drew knew how to read a contract and extract its exact meaning. He had become an expert at this type of "coverage opinion" over the years and it was good work, but not exactly scintillating. The morning passed slowly with no call from Rick.

At precisely 1:00 his cell phone rang. It was Rick, who was in Huntsville and asked if Drew could meet him in Birmingham for dinner. Birmingham lies about half way between Huntsville and Drew's home in Tuscaloosa. Drew checked his calendar and they agreed to meet that evening at 7:00. Rick never mentioned the pictures, so neither did he.

Drew left a few minutes late because he remembered that he had promised his wife that he would pick up their dog at the vet. So, after dropping off the dog at home, he drove his BMW 535i faster than usual up the interstate to Birmingham. He parked and trotted into the restaurant outside the Galleria mall still wearing his usual office attire of khaki slacks and button-down dress shirt.

After surveying the diners from the front of the restaurant, Drew's phone dinged announcing he had a text. It read, "I'm in a booth near the back. Left side."

Relieved because he wasn't exactly sure he could pick Rick out from the other diners after several weeks, Drew walked over.

Rick noticed Drew enter the restaurant, but trying to avoid calling extra attention to himself, didn't wave him over. Instead, he sent Drew a quick text. His thoughts were occupied by what he could tell Drew that would both explain his note about needing help, but prevent Drew from getting nervous. He lied when he wrote that the pictures of the GW-1 weren't classified. In fact everything about the GW-1 was highly classified. He took the very slight chance that Drew would show the pictures to someone else because he needed this lawyer to be intrigued enough to meet with him. Even if Drew allowed the pictures to get out, rumors of an ultra high-speed aircraft with a triangular shape were already making their way through the aerospace world, and debates were taking place in popular media over whether they were

UFOs or some advanced military plane. But so far, so good.

Approaching the table Drew thought Rick looked uneasy, but dismissed the thought, writing it off as social discomfort. He remembered Rick as friendly, but somewhat shy, except when talking about his work. Drew shook Rick's hand as he slid into the opposite side of the wide booth.

"Good to see you again. Thanks for the pictures. Very cool. How have you been?"

"Good, thanks. Nice to see you again, too. Thanks for meeting me. I don't know anyone in Huntsville and I thought, well, since I'm in Alabama…. Anyway, I really appreciate you driving up here to meet me."

Drew noticed that Rick glanced around the restaurant as he spoke.

"Expecting someone else?" Drew asked.

"Oh, uh, no. Sorry. It's just been a long day," Rick said shaking his head. "How about a beer?" Rick asked just as the waiter had arrived at the table. Drew declined the beer but ordered a glass of Chianti.

"I'm glad you called, but I confess I'm a little baffled. We meet on a plane and have a nice conversation. Then I get some pictures of airplanes, a note asking for help, and an invitation to dinner. Maybe I've read too many spy novels, but is there something going on I need to know about?" Drew asked in a light-hearted manner.

Rick looked at Drew and then let out a small chuckle. "No, no. Nothing like that. I didn't mean to create a mystery at all. I just need some help with a personal project. I'll fill you in if you don't mind talking a little business."

Drew couldn't help being just a little disappointed. Some small part of him had hoped Rick might want his help on a secret project or something exciting. Of course he knew this wouldn't be the case, but Rick had worked at Area 51, after all!

"Sure," Drew agreed and then added remembering Rick lived in Maryland, "I don't know the first thing about Maryland law, but I'll help if I can. What's going on?"

"Well its really fairly straightforward. I'm thinking about opening up a business of my own here in Alabama."

"I see. Setting up a corporation or LLC for you is no problem at all. But why Alabama? You live and work in Maryland, right?" Drew inquired.

"That's right, for now, but Alabama has one of the largest concentrations of technology companies in the country. I'm thinking about leaving Pratt and maybe moving down here. And, I grew up in South Carolina. I'd love to move back to the South." Rick didn't tell Drew he had left Pratt & Whitney months ago. "In fact, to be honest, that's really my plan right now. Pratt's a great company, but I think I've gone as far as I can with them. Besides, I've got some ideas that customers down here might find interesting. Any contacts I can make in Alabama would be helpful. What do you think?"

"Well, I don't have any contacts in the world of technology or aerospace, but I can help get a business set up. I wouldn't mind a break from insurance law anyway. So, sure. Why not? If I don't have the know-how to do something you need, I'll let you know," Drew answered. "I'd have to charge you by the hour for any legal work though. My high-end, jet-set lifestyle in Tuscaloosa, Alabama, demands exorbitant fees. "

Rick snickered. "Of course, of course, Your Honor. I wouldn't expect otherwise," Rick said trying to put Drew at ease by matching his sarcasm. "I've set aside some funds for you as a retainer and you can bill against that for now." Rick reached into his shirt pocket and laid a cashier's check for $25,000 made out to Drew on the table. "I went ahead and got this in case you agreed to represent me, or in case you needed convincing."

"Wow! Consider me convinced!" Drew said, reaching across the table and shaking Rick's hand. "You've got yourself a lawyer."

They spent the rest of the evening eating and getting to know each other. Rick was a thirty-seven-year-old bachelor. His only real interests were engineering and aerospace. He told Drew he had been working at Pratt & Whitney ever since receiving his doctorate in applied aerospace engineering from MIT.

During his career, Rick had risen quickly in the company, becoming instrumental in the development of power units for all types of aircraft, but specializing in military applications. Being single with few outside interests or expensive tastes, Rick had been able to invest the vast majority of his pay for past fifteen years. Money was no longer a worry for him.

Looking at Rick, one would never believe he was a genius aerospace engineer. He wore a short-sleeve plaid button-down shirt, generic jeans, and plain leather loafers. In fact, he looked and acted more like the manager of a CVS drugstore than a rocket scientist. Rick could be flighty, but he also clearly loved his work. Drew had to remind himself that engineers and scientists were like artists, often entirely focused on their work and just as entirely unconcerned with social convention.

After dinner, they walked out to the parking lot together. Rick asked Drew to accompany him to his car so he could give Rick a packet of documents. Drew didn't really think about why, but Rick had parked at the back of the parking lot and away from the overhead lamps. Rick opened the trunk and pulled out a thick plain manila-shipping envelope sealed with packing tape.

"This is some of my plans, computer code and stuff like that. You have a safe?" Rick asked.

"Sure." Drew said with a slight hesitation in his voice. "Is there something I need to know about this? I'm not holding something hot am I?" Drew asked. "We should be clear. I won't be part of anything illegal whatsoever. I don't want to seem paranoid, but I have to be sure."

Rick once again chuckled. "No, no, no. This is nothing more than a duplicate copy of my own ideas, the backup of my backup in old-school hard copy form. I want to keep it with someone I trust and somewhere safe. Competition in the aerospace industry is cutthroat and I just want to be able to prove that stuff is actually mine. I have some things to wrap up for P&W and then I'll be in touch. You can look at it you want, but unless you have an advanced engineering degree, I don't think you'd find it too interesting."

While still just a little wary, Drew had to admit Rick's explanation made sense. Why would Rick give him permission to look through the documents if they were somehow questionable? Plus, twenty-five grand would make a nice bonus—once he earned it, of course. For now, the money would just sit in his firm's bank trust account. So, Drew took the packet, shook Rick's hand again and headed toward his car.

After Drew left, Rick closed the trunk and got in his rented Chevrolet Camaro. But he didn't drive off immediately. He just sat there, completely still for several minutes, his hand shaking from adrenaline release. It had taken monumental effort to maintain a calm and friendly demeanor during dinner. Rick suspected he had been followed earlier in the day. If that was true, he was dead and Drew would have a hell of a time explaining why he had plans for the most advanced aircraft in the world and its integrated gravity-wave propulsion system. Rick didn't enjoy using Drew like this. He liked Drew. But he needed a safety net, one he could trust with his life. Once calm, he drove out of Birmingham, heading east.

EIGHT

Two years ago

Dr. Rick Donnelly brimmed with nerdish delight. Nothing got Rick's blood pumping like state-of-the-art technology and engineering. And today, he stood inside the singularly unique and ultimately exclusive facility where "state of the art" was considered only a starting point.

Over the past sixty years, Groom Lake, also popularly known as Area 51, housed and nurtured physicists, engineers, chemists, and others at the spear point of technological innovation. The work undertaken at Area 51 produced results far ahead of humanity's expectations. If the public knew half of the advancements achieved within this remote complex, the fabric of society itself might be in jeopardy. So, for over fifty years, the government didn't even acknowledge that Area 51 existed.

Located about a hundred miles northeast of Las Vegas, Nevada, Area 51 occupies a portion of remote Nevada desert twenty-three miles wide and twenty-five miles long. Signs located on the few dusty roads leading to Area 51 warn potential intruders that they will be met with "deadly force." The government picked this deserted part of the Nevada Test Range, the site of many nuclear weapons tests during the 1950s, for its inaccessibility. The nearest town, Rachel, Nevada, is forty-five miles away and has a permanent population of less than thirty people. Those working at Area 51 fly to and from the facility on unmarked white and orange airliners out of the Las Vegas airport. Open control tower communications refer these as "Janet flights." Groom Lake belongs, at least nominally, to the Air Force. But every branch of the United States' military and many civilian companies use this isolated and lonely location to redefine the word "impossible."

The ultra-secrecy of Area 51 has stoked the imagination of conspiracy theorists and UFO nuts for decades. They accuse the government of everything up to and including working directly with living extraterrestrial beings within the clandestine facility. Claims of UFO sightings over or around the base occur so frequently that few people really pay attention any more. Rick Donnelly knew all about Groom Lake's mystique; and, he knew it was all crap.

Donnelly traveled to Groom Lake after the Air Force urgently requested Rick's assistance from his employer, Pratt & Whitney. The United States Senate Appropriations Subcommittee on Defense had ordered the Air Force to submit the final prototype of the new YF-26 fighter/bomber for final funding consideration. Several important members of the subcommittee would be at Ellis Air Force Base in California for a demonstration. With just weeks until the all-important exhibition, the new plane's two Pratt & Whitney J-97 engines had to meet or exceed all performance specifications—without fail.

The Klass -Tyros

Pratt & Whitney deployed Rick to Area 51 to implement his newly perfected method of maintaining the hundreds of compressor blades contained in the company's most advanced military engines. Like all jet engines, the efficiency and power of the J-97s depended on the precise angle of its compressor fins and their alignment to one another. Before Rick's innovation, engines had to be removed from the aircraft, disassembled, and the vanes aligned by hand using highly accurate table jigs. Rick developed a way to test and realign the blades without removing the engine from the aircraft. Using Rick's procedure, jet engines could be returned to peak performance in two hours. The usual method required at least twenty.

Despite its vast size, Area 51 has limited capacity and the projects given access to its unique facilities have the highest priority; so research and development work take place twenty-four hours a day. Rick's tight schedule required very long and unusual hours. But, thanks to his invention and prodigy-level engineering talent, the YF-26's two J-97 engines far surpassed the power output the original designers of the engines had considered possible. This fact most assuredly pleased the military brass, who would, for once, get more than they asked for. But, Rick would soon learn his technological masterpiece was on the verge of becoming obsolete.

Shortly before Rick was to leave Nevada and return to Pratt & Whitney's home office in New Jersey, Rick bore witness to the impossible.

At about 2:00 AM Rick left building B-7, one of Area 51's above ground hangars, which housed the two YF-26 prototypes. To anyone looking at the base from the ground, or more likely from space, the above ground facilities would appear profoundly plain, even shabby. But these hangars were not only used to house operational and near operational aircraft, they also provided perfect camouflage for the six immense elevators that provided access to the majority of the facility. Area 51 was actually a multi-level city of huge hangars, laboratories, testing space, offices, and living quarters dug deep into the Nevada desert. Secure from even the most invasive surveillance technologies, a vast network of tunnels, some wide and tall enough to move two B-52 bombers through side by side, connected the subterranean spaces.

Donnelly usually took the elevator in B-7 down to Level 4 and then rode the monorail mag-lev tram back to his temporary quarters. But tonight, he needed to get outside and breathe some fresh air. He decided to walk down the flight line outside before making his way to the cafeteria for some breakfast—or whatever one might call a meal at 2:00 AM.

Once outside, Rick found the night cooler than expected, but the view of the distant mountain ranges lit by moonlight to the east and west in the crystal clear air of the desert made up for the slight chill. On nights like this, the blanket of stars overhead revealed the infinite depth of the universe. Maryland never offered up nights like this. A long, deep breath left him feeling amazingly refreshed and the fact that his work was coming to a successful conclusion further buoyed his excellent mood. After taking time to enjoy the moment, he stuck his hands in the pockets of his white lab coat, turned right, and walked by the enormous closed main door of Hangar B-7.

Since the military and its contractors regularly tested "black" project aircraft and equipment at night; movement outside was often prohibited. The Air Force Special Operations Unit, or Spec Ops, furnished Area 51's armed security. Spec Ops personnel left no doubt when a base-wide lockdown was scheduled. While sensitive testing took place outside, Spec Ops personnel stood guard at every exit. Anyone unwary enough to approach an exterior door during a lockdown would be ordered once, and only once, to move away. The Spec Ops guard would give this command from behind his locked, loaded, and aimed HK416 assault rifle. Rick had very carefully confirmed that Spec Ops had not announced a lockdown tonight before heading outside.

Rick felt like a million bucks. But, just as he passed the open area between Hangars B-6 and B-5, a violent, swirling wall of wind and sand assaulted him from the right. The gust grabbed at his clothes; causing him to throw his arm up to cover his face and to take two steps sideways just to stay upright. Then, as suddenly as it began, the onslaught vanished. Rick first blamed the sometimes-unpredictable desert environment, but the thought vanished as he looked back between the two huge buildings.

Less than fifty yards away a huge triangular aircraft rose silently into the air. Its nose pointed directly at Rick and he could clearly see its outline against the night sky. He was astonished, dumbfounded even, by this craft. *It had no visible engines*! But, the lack of engines was not its most curious feature. Not even close.

The aircraft continued to ascend straight up. As the angle of his view changed, Rick could make out its entire underside. Where one might expect engine pods or intakes on the wings, this craft had two round holes. *Holes?* Rick questioned what he was seeing. *But, yes, he could see completely through both wings into the night sky! Was this the propulsion system? Was there a crew? What the hell?* Rick's mind became overwhelmed with questions it couldn't answer. He stood as if his shoes were nailed into the ground. He couldn't take his eyes off what he was seeing.

When the vehicle reached an altitude of about one thousand feet, it yawed left in a completely flat rotation around its center axis. As he watched, it stopped, hung absolutely motionless in the air for a few seconds, and then began rotating again, this time to its right. Then, in an unparalleled and seemingly impossible maneuver, the craft pitched up until it stood on its tail. After pausing briefly with its nose pointed straight up, the plane slowly continued the maneuver until it turned all the way over onto its back. Once again it stopped, absolutely still, upside down. After flipping once again back to its original position, the craft suddenly and silently shot forward.

Before he could blink, it disappeared over one of the mountain ranges Rick knew to be over fifteen miles from where he stood.

Shaken to his core, even Rick's doctorate in aerospace engineering couldn't help him find an explanation for this apparition. Until this moment, he believed he and his company were at the cutting edge of aircraft propulsion systems. But in just the last few minutes he grasped the fact that they were several orders of technological magnitude behind whatever powered that thing.

Rick had to fight off his near catatonic state. Thinking he must have inadvertently broken security, he hurried on to the next hangar and down an elevator to the cafeteria. But nobody confronted him or mentioned a classified flight. His mind still preoccupied trying to make sense of how the craft could maneuver the way it did, he found himself walking slowly past some tables with a cup of coffee in his hand. As he walked, sipping at his coffee, someone called out, "Hey, Rick! You're up late boy!"

Rick looked up and saw Dr. Dave Knox, one of the Lockheed Skunk Works engineers he had worked with for a day or so on the YF-26. Dave was one of those guys that liked everyone and everyone liked him. He was from somewhere in Georgia, Rick couldn't remember where exactly, but he knew Dave was one of the finest aerospace engineers in the country. The Skunk Works only hired the best for its ultra-advanced projects.

Knox sat at a round table with one other man and they both seemed quite pleased with themselves. "Come on over and take a load off," Dave suggested waving him over. "This here is Nate Sanford. Nate, Rick Donnelly. Rick's the guy that developed the in-craft vane alignment procedure for P and W. Good stuff."

Obviously a nerd's nerd, Sanford wore a white, short-sleeve, button-down shirt complete with pocket protector. "Nice to meet you," Dave's friend said in a disturbingly nasally voice while getting up from the table. "Sorry, but I have to review tonight's data points before tomorrow's performance review committee. Nice work on your engines. Sorry it won't be needed much longer."

Nate walked away and Rick sat down across from Dave. "What did he mean by that?" Rick asked.

"Oh, don't mind 'ol Nate. He's OK, just ain't got much social skill, if you know what I mean," Dave replied, dismissing Nate's jab as unintended. "He's talking about tonight's test. What'd you think?"

"What?" Rick said not understanding. "What do you mean?"

"The test you just saw. What did you think?" Dave repeated, smiling.

"Oh. Yeah," Rick responded uncomfortably. "Well, you know, uh, I just saw something I hope I wasn't supposed to. Honest to God, if I didn't know better, I would have to say I'd seen a flying saucer."

"Ah! Then you were impressed. Good. So here's the thing," Dave said enthusiastically. "You were supposed to see that test. In fact, I arranged it so you would. What did you think? Awesome, right?"

"Yeah. Oh, yeah!" Rick said finally catching up with Dave's cryptic questions. "What was that? What kind of propulsion system does it have? It's beyond wild! And, wait a minute, what do you mean you arranged for me to see, this, uh, test?" Rick obviously wanted to know everything. Dave could see Rick was hooked.

Dave explained, "That was the GW-FB1, our newest creation. The guys at the Works are impressed with your vane alignment process, but more to the point, your ability to think outside the box. To innovate. We arranged for you to see an operational test of the Gravity Wave Fighter Bomber One. We need guys like you on our team. What do you think?"

It took just a moment for Knox's statement to sink in. "Are you telling me that plane utilizes gravity wave propulsion?" Rick blurted, almost too loudly.

"Yes sir. Gravity ain't just good for dropping a crap anymore."

NINE

After that night at Area 51, Rick Donnelly joined Lockheed Martin as a senior aerospace engineer and designer. He became part of the legendary Skunk Works, the hyper-advanced division of Lockheed Martin created by Kelly Johnson and responsible for revolutionary aircraft such as the U-2, SR-1 Blackbird, and F-22 Raptor. Assigned to the GW-FB1's propulsion system team, Rick's first task was to master the science of gravity waves. Over the next several months, the prototype continued its test cycles while Rick gained a deep understanding of the gravity wave reactor—how it was fueled and the techniques for gravity wave projection and manipulation. Utilizing his PhDs in aerospace engineering and theoretical physics, Rick quickly helped thrust the technology forward.

Within his first six months with Lockheed, Rick re-designed the propulsion unit's gravity wave reflector, a complex modulation circuit that minimized wave reduction by nearly 40 percent as it dispersed around the craft's body. Rick's instinctive ability to overcome problems and conceive novel advances earned him a spot on the small team led by Dr. Dave Knox, developing and producing the complex fuel needed for the gravity wave reactor. While the element necessary for sustained gravity wave propulsion had been created years before, the job of creating the process to produce the element in sufficient quantity fell to Knox's team.

While they worked closely with two other brilliant scientists, it was Rick and Dave who eventually conceived the needed production method. Developing a close friendship, Dave and Rick spent any free time they had together; despite the fact that they worked long hours in the same lab. Their respective talents and backgrounds made them naturally compatible, despite their disparate personalities.

Rick's grandmother raised him after his mother and father divorced just before Rick turned three years old. After the divorce, his father disappeared into the backwoods, some said to drink himself to death. Rick's mother left town with another man. Rick's grandmother blamed her ex-daughter-in-law for destroying her only son and told anyone who would listen that Rick's mother ended up a prostitute in Nevada. Whatever the truth, neither ever returned to claim their son.

Rick and his grandmother lived in a small community outside of Columbia, South Carolina, and Rick attended county schools nearby. Ms. Donnelly, as everyone in the neighborhood called Rick's grandmother, retired from the tire manufacturing plant when Rick was ten. A strict Southern Baptist, Ms. Donnelly did not drink, smoke, or use foul language. She maintained strict control over every aspect of Rick's life, raising him as she had been raised, with iron discipline and the Holy Bible. Ms. Donnelly was also a non-repentant and outspoken bigot, holding a grudge from the time President Johnson forced her small county high school to accept black students.

Rick's overbearing grandmother and his extremely high IQ, which became evident while he was still in elementary school, made him an outcast in his lower-middle class neighborhood. As a result of all this, Rick lacked social skills, kept to himself, and concentrated on his true love—science. The almost immeasurable capability of Rick's mind eventually released him from his plain, boring, and often emotionally painful life. High school offered young Rick no challenge, even though he skipped two grades and graduated before his seventeenth birthday. His perfect score on the ACT college entrance exam and the highest possible grade point average attracted college recruiters from universities all over the country offering impressive scholarships.

Rick finally chose the Massachusetts Institute of Technology because of its well-known leadership in aerospace engineering and astronautics. Ms. Donnelly didn't approve of studying science or, for that matter, Massachusetts. Both went against her religion, or so she steadfastly claimed. But Rick's desire for knowledge and the challenge of MIT outweighed his grandmother's strong opinions and Rick's guilt about leaving her. Despite her flagrant disregard for political correctness, her bristly personality and her penchant for quoting the Old Testament, Rick loved his grandmother.

Rick didn't understand the strong racial opinions held by Ms. Donnelly, but he did become wary of government intervention in peoples' lives. If he had been publicly outspoken, he would have expressed the opinion that government should get out of the way and allow science to progress unmolested. He felt that most politicians had mediocre minds and were profoundly unqualified to judge the work done by leading scientists, engineers, and doctors. But other than that, he paid no attention to politics or the news in general. They wasted his time.

Rick's college career was entirely academic. He had no interest in a social life and never even considered joining a fraternity. Excelling at MIT, he eventually became one of the youngest postgraduate students to earn two doctorate degrees. While he could have continued as a professor at MIT or almost any other major university, Rick instead accepted a lucrative job offer from Pratt & Whitney. During his six years in Cambridge, Rick visited Ms. Donnelly only a handful of times. While he felt considerable remorse about often ignoring his only family, he also had a difficult time tolerating his grandmother's criticism and attempts to steer his life.

Dave Knox, meanwhile, grew up in Claxton, Georgia, a small town about forty miles west of Savannah.

Dave's parents both taught in the Evans County School District and Dave attended Claxton Elementary, Junior High and High School. After showing signs of extreme intelligence early in life, his parents devoted themselves to nurturing his gifts. They doted on him, foregoing many comforts to purchase private courses for gifted students. Along with a brilliant mind, Dave was a natural, even charismatic, leader. He played quarterback for the Claxton Tigers and served as president of his senior class. After high school, he chose to attend Georgia Tech in Atlanta on a full academic scholarship.

Dave joined Eta Mu fraternity as an incoming freshman. The fraternity's officers immediately recognized Dave as a great asset. While never seeking election himself, Dave used his talent for attracting friends and influencing people to help his frat brothers and The Tyros organization to victory in student government elections. His efforts gained him membership into a secret committee of other fraternity leaders who actually ran The Tyros. It was no surprise to Dave when he learned that a group of influential alumni actually managed The Tyros through the Chairman of the committee. He was told these alumni were referred to as "The Doyens." The Chairman received both advice and orders from The Doyens and implemented their edicts through committee members.

Dave became indispensible to the Chairman, carrying out orders without question and always obtaining results beyond what was expected. On one occasion, Dave pursued and formed a relationship with one of the editors of the student newspaper, *The Technique*, solely for the purpose of persuading her The Tyros was nothing more than a bunch of irrepressible frat boys who should be ignored. The young editor, completely smitten, authored an editorial comparing any obsession with The Tyros with Don Quixote's obsession with windmills.

Dave's diligence and talent did not escape notice by The Doyens.

TEN

During the last week of his junior year at Georgia Tech, Dave received an unexpected invitation to meet one of The Doyens in person. Instructed to wear a jacket and that the meeting was nobody else's business, he was to be at the Sundial restaurant at the top of the Peachtree Plaza Hotel in downtown Atlanta at a specific date and time. Dave arrived ten minutes early and rode the glass elevator up to the rotating restaurant on the top floor. As he walked toward the restaurant entrance, a sharply dressed attendant looked up and immediately approached him.

"Mr. Knox, welcome. Your host is waiting in our private dining area. This way, please." Without further explanation, he led Dave to a private room with immense floor-to-ceiling windows framing an imposing view of downtown Atlanta that seemed to creep across glass. Upon entering, Dave encountered a single elegantly laid window table at which sat a dignified looking gentleman sipping a crystal tumbler of unidentified light brown liquor.

The maître d' announced, "Your guest has arrived, sir." He then turned, and politely exited.

The Doyen looked to be in his early sixties. His deeply tanned face and the few lines it displayed lent considerable gravitas. Bright blue eyes peered from beneath heavy gray eyebrows and thick gray hair flowed back over the top of his head and behind his ears.

Impeccably dressed in a tailored dark blue suit, pinpoint oxford cloth shirt, and solid red tie, he looked up and smiled, brandishing astonishingly white teeth.

"Come in son, come in. I've been looking forward to our meeting. Please have a seat," The Doyen invited, waiving vaguely at the single lavishly upholstered chair across the table.

Dave had never experienced first-class dining. Another young man from Claxton, Georgia, might have felt uncomfortable, but not Dave. He wasn't intimidated or impressed easily, but he had to admit to himself that this whole thing oozed awesomeness.

"Thank you," Dave said pulling out his chair. "And thank you for the invitation. This is an unexpected honor." Dave sat down. The distinguished gentleman across the table had not offered his hand, or introduced himself, so Dave did the same.

"I hear you enjoy a glass of fine wine from time to time. So, I've taken the liberty of ordering a bottle for us. I hope you approve," The Doyen said, motioning for someone to enter.

The door opened and the sommelier entered the room and presented a bottle of wine to The Doyen, who nodded. After pouring each an exacting amount into their glasses, the sommelier placed the bottle on the table and left.

Dave did enjoy visiting local wine shops and purchasing a nice bottle from time to time. He found wine far more interesting than beer or liquor, but he stuck to beer in public for appearances sake. It was somewhat telling that The Doyen mentioned this little known fact right off the bat. While no expert, yet, Dave certainly recognized the world famous "Petrus" label adorning the bottle now on the table. He would later look up its price and find it sold for over $1,500.

Dave took a sip, allowing the deep garnet-colored liquid to sit on his tongue for a moment. He had never tasted anything like it! There was no doubt in his mind— *this is how he wanted to live!*

The Doyen picked up his glass and took a long disinterested swallow, as if drinking thousand-dollar bottles of wine at lunch was ordinary, even mundane. Dave politely let The Doyen begin the conversation.

"Mr. Knox, I've heard very good things about you. I have been informed of your service to your fraternity, Tech, and The Tyros. You also have the highest grade point average attainable. Your professors report that you possess beyond-genius level intelligence and, more importantly, you can use your gifts effectively. Quite impressive indeed. I can see you know how to handle yourself. I have not even introduced myself, or told you the reason you are here. Yet, you sit here quite comfortably," The Doyen said impassively.

Dave responded, "Thank you for your kind words. I very much enjoy everything I do at Tech. At the risk of seeming conceited, I must admit I am confident in my abilities. But that doesn't mean I don't strive to improve. As for your identity, I know you are one of The Doyens that help guide The Tyros. Therefore, you are most likely an alumnus of Tech. But other than that inference, I have no other information about you, sir. And, I see no need to try making further deductions along those lines. So, the setting is beautiful and the view is truly exquisite, but if I may ask, why am I here?"

The Doyen nodded, studying Dave closely before responding gregariously. "Of course, of course Mr. Knox! Your curiosity is to be expected. I'll come to the point. The Doyens have decided to offer you the chairmanship of The Tyros' control committee at Georgia Tech should you agree to our terms. I have asked you here to gauge your interest and explain what that position requires and what it can do for you." The Doyen continued. "What I'm about to tell you is confidential, and we must ask you not to reveal this to anyone, or make further inquiries yourself. We are quite serious in this regard. So if you wish to continue this conversation you must give me your word that you will not do either thing."

"Sir, you do have my word. I'll stand on my actions to date to back that up," Dave answered immediately.

"Alright then. The Doyens, as we were named decades ago, are not just student advisors helping universities' Greek societies win elections out of old loyalty to our fraternities. The Tyros, at Tech and other Southern universities, is actually part of a much larger organization of prominent business people, professionals, politicians, and others, who have acquired the resources to wield a significant amount of influence in various areas."

The Doyen gauged Dave's reaction. Apparently satisfied, he continued. "The Doyens have two tasks. The first is to collaborate, on behalf of themselves and many others, to effect positive change in society, government, and the economy while protecting our own, shall we call it, place in society. It is our organization's simple belief that those with ability, drive, and ambition provide, through their efforts, the necessary resources demanded by the remainder of the population. In short, without the employment opportunities, financial organizations, and services we create, the economy and thus society itself would crumble. Protection of our class status is essential, not just for us, but for the country as a whole. Second, we are asked to see that the generation following ours is prepared to carry on our work. I am here today on the second of those tasks. Do you have any concerns about what I've said so far?" The Doyen paused, allowing Dave a chance to respond.

"None at all sir. I'm intrigued. Please go on," Dave replied.

The Doyen nodded and continued. "As I said, one of The Doyens' jobs is to assure that the next generation is prepared to take over this organization. Since the founding of this country, men of superior talent have created wealth through entrepreneurism, fearless risk taking, and unbridled drive. However, as long as men have worked to create wealth for themselves and opportunity for others, opposing forces have tried to usurp their efforts, attempting to wring as much money as possible out of their pockets and into public coffers. I'll offer some well-known examples. In 1833, President Andrew Jackson vetoed a re-charter of the Second National Bank of the United States, withdrew the nation's currency and placed it into what they called his "pet banks." His actions destroyed the most powerful private financial institution in the country. President Lincoln used force to ruin the Planter Class of the South, setting the economy of the South back decades. President Theodore Roosevelt used the power of government to break up private corporations in the steel, oil, and railroad industries. Ah, but now I seem to have gotten on my soapbox, so I shall step down. My point being that our class must remain strong against government overreach, most particularly the federal government's efforts to take away the life we have built for ourselves."

Dave already knew and understood the historical references. Opinions concerning the reasons for those governmental actions varied, but the outcome of each could not be debated. Dave wanted to know more about this "organization."

"I believe I understand," Dave said. "Your organization works to guard the entire class of business owners, entrepreneurs, professionals, and so on by producing and maintaining counter-pressure against the government. I imagine this is accomplished by many methods. But, since the government never dies, your organization must continuously revitalize itself. Quite brilliant really."

"Absolutely correct. You really don't disappoint, do you Mr. Knox?" The Doyen asked rhetorically. "We have existed as an organization for many decades, and with your help, we shall continue to do so."

"I'd like to be of as much assistance to you as possible," Dave responded.

"Very good. All right then. As a general rule, Chairman of The Tyros come from wealthy, influential families. Families with assets to protect. This incentivizes the young man to work diligently. While you don't have that background, you have other gifts, gifts you wish to exploit to the fullest. We feel that your ambition and talent overcome your current lack of social standing and family assets. With that said, The Chairman has two jobs. The first is to carry out direction from The Doyens, to be our strong right hand where needed to run The Tyros. The other is to identify and develop promising younger men who may be able to take over from you. Sound familiar?" Dave nodded and The Doyen continued. "Remember this, one must first have loyalty to and learn from his superiors if he, himself, is one day to advance into a superior position himself."

The Doyen stopped talking for a moment; becoming quite serious. "Now, I must ask the most important question of the afternoon. What The Doyens ask and require is quite onerous, but the rewards far outweigh the cost. Our instructions must be performed without question and to the letter. Every time. Should you agree, we will expect just that level of commitment, so please think carefully. Breaking your word to us can have consequences as unpleasant as the rewards are fabulous. So, knowing the terms, will you make that commitment and accept the chairmanship for Georgia Tech? Please, take your time."

Dave's answer was never in doubt, but he carefully considered everything he was just told anyway. While he felt he could certainly be a success in any aerospace firm, "success" was not enough. Dave wanted a life in which he, like the man sitting before him, could ascend to a position of real power and wealth. Looking back at The Doyen, Dave said with confidence, "You have my word, my loyalty, and my obedience. Without reservation."

The Doyen studied Dave's face, looking for any hint of deception. There was none.

"Excellent. Now we can get to the nuts and bolts," The Doyen said reaching into his pocket and removing a thick plain white envelope. He placed it on the table and pushed it across the pristine white tablecloth toward Dave, but kept his hand on the envelope as he continued speaking. "We shall call this a scholarship. Please use it as such. You will also find within a telephone number. Enter that number into your phone as a contact. Use the name William Simmons. Keep your phone within reach and charged twenty-four hours a day. If it rings identifying Mr. Simmons as the caller, answer, listen, and act as instructed," The Doyen said, placing his hand back on his wine glass and gesturing for Dave to take the envelope with the other.

Only now did Dave pick up the envelope and place it in his jacket pocket—without looking at it or its contents. "Yes, sir. Understood," he replied.

"Good. Keep The Tyros in power, develop new talent and follow instructions. Do well, as I know you will, and the scholarship you just received will look quite insignificant indeed," The Doyen instructed, picking up his menu for the first time. "Our business is concluded, thank you for coming, the maître d' will collect you."

The Doyen didn't look up again. It was plainly time to leave.

Dave stood, and without another word passing between them he left, escorted by the maître d'. Dave savored his surroundings as he walked out. He noted that the rotation of the restaurant revealed a whole new horizon from the one presented when he first entered.

Only after getting into his old Honda Accord in the hotel's parking deck did Dave open the envelope. Inside, he found $10,000 in neatly stacked and banded one hundred dollar bills. As instructed, he entered a contact for William Simmons into his phone. Despite his vast intelligence, he didn't take time to consider all the possible ramifications of the commitment he just made, or to whom he just swore allegiance.

Through the next year, Dave's governance of The Tyros at Georgia Tech would prove to be nothing less than masterful, matched only by his loyalty to The Doyens and their organization. The Doyens in turn, rewarded him generously. After successfully advancing the next Chairman into his position, Dave continued at Georgia Tech, where he earned a doctorate in aerospace engineering. Lockheed Martin recruited him quickly and at extravagant expense.

Over the years Dr. David Knox returned to Georgia from time to time to meet with The Doyens and occasionally see his parents. While in Atlanta, he often made it a point to have lunch at the Sundial.

ELEVEN

Present Day

Hunter Dodson, *"the third" nonetheless*, had irritated Jimbo with the assignment of cleaning out certain competition to The Tyros. Dodson selected him to scare an independent candidate for president of the SGA badly enough so that she withdrew from the election. He normally would have been excited, and even honored, to take on an important job for The Tyros and he knew he could have handled this one easily. But Dodson also had ordered him to use The Boys, which he believed to be massive overkill and a big pain in the butt.

The Boys were not members of any fraternity, or even students. They were the "black sheep" of moneyed and important families, the same families whose offspring joined The Tyros. Some had tried college, but couldn't be bothered with grades. The rich environment of parties, drugs, and girls that college life offered took priority. Once their parents realized that college was a waste of time and money, most pulled their funding (at least for college), forcing their offspring into finding other ways to occupy their time. Some of The Boys lived at home, sponging off their parents, while others took minimal jobs or earned extra cash in the illegal drug industry. Most of The Boys did all of these things. Like members of The Tyros, they had been indoctrinated to believe in their superiority and their right to a privileged lifestyle. The Doyens ensured The Boys contributed to their objectives according to their unique talents.

The Boys banded together, refusing to associate with the lower classes. They weren't a gang, as such, but more a loose club, willing to perform necessary jobs requiring violence, crime, or lack of morality. They were akin to skinheads or Neo-Nazis, but with much better breeding. The Boys underwent military-style combat training by ex-special forces operatives, paid for and arranged by The Doyens. Favorite classes included instruction in advanced firearms, hand-to-hand combat, and of course, explosives. The Boys were certainly dangerous, but they also took and obeyed orders. Their contribution was often violent and messy.

J.P. Hoffman led The Boys as their current First Man. The First Man was not appointed or elected. Any of The Boys could become First Man by physically beating the incumbent so that he had to be hospitalized for over three days. The rules of succession prohibited a challenger from using weapons of any kind, but did not keep the ambitious challenger from attacking the First Man without warning. This draconian arrangement kept the First Man constantly on guard and careful to know as much as possible about each individual member, their whereabouts and activities. Conversely, it motivated the membership to be physically tough and watchful for any weakness in the First Man.

J.P. had enjoyed a long reign as First Man. Over two years ago he pulled then First Man "Dog" Albright off the top of a naked, squealing, drunk trailer-trash white girl. Dog created his own disadvantage because his jeans were down around his ankles. J.P. just opened the door to Dog's truck and pulled him out by his feet. Dog was tough, but a quick kick to his testicles, as he tried to get up on his knees, took the fight out of him. Dog was still face down and with his hands locked around his crotch when J.P. dropped a knee onto Dog's left upper arm, breaking the humerus in two places. Dog didn't scream in pain only because the shot to his scrotum had forced all the breath out of his body. J.P. then had time to consider his options. The arm probably wouldn't require three days in the hospital, so he decided on three kicks to the head to induce a nice concussion. It worked. Three days later he was the new First Man.

Dog stayed pissed off for a long time, but now he was J.P.'s right-hand man and second in command. J.P. knew all about keeping his friends close and his enemies even closer.

J.P.'s position as First Man came loaded with privileges. He received a generous allowance from The Doyens, which he could spend as he wished. Members gave him first choice of women; and, liquor, pot and blow were all free. Truly the good life. Other members had challenged him three times, each a miserable failure. J.P. was considerably smarter than almost every other member and nobody could match his fighting skill. But it was his ability to keep track of the members, gain information on any planned attack, and prepare continuously that kept him on top. His challenge to Dog represented a perfect case in point. J.P. knew Dog's weakness: Dog's brain turned off when he screwed. A man who turns his back and drops his pants makes an easy target.

Despite his considerable exasperation, Jimbo called J.P. and set a meeting. Jimbo and J.P. had attended the same private high school and played football on the same team. Jimbo played tight end and J.P. played cornerback; so they ran into each other regularly at practice. They weren't friends then or now, so J.P. knew something was up as soon as Jimbo called.

Jimbo explained what they needed. "We have to scare the hell out of someone. And I'm talkin' about scarin' her bad. Her name is Mary O'Dell, she's runnin' for president and she lives by herself just off campus. We need her out of the elections. I'm open to ideas."

"Just scared? That's all?" J.P. asked.

"Yeah, just scared. That's it. This ain't fun time for The Boys. This is important to the The Doyens, so don't screw it up. Just make sure she knows she has to get out of the race and right goddamn now. It's up to you how you get this done. Keep control of your men and don't get caught."

J.P. thought about it for a minute, coming up with a quick plan. "We'll follow her for a couple of days to see when she's most likely to be alone. We'll do the job, probably Thursday night if an opportunity presents itself.

By Monday y'all will be unopposed, guaranteed. You want to come along?"

"I have to. Orders. But I'll stay out of the action. I'm supposed to stay invisible. I'll be around to be sure it goes smooth and quiet, with no problems," Jimbo stated, trying to sound in charge.

"Don't get your pretty panties all up your butt, Jimbo. Couldn't be easier. I'll let you know when it's set."

That Thursday night, Jimbo waited for J.P. in the parking lot of the Camellia Gardens Apartments, one of the many small off-campus complexes rented exclusively to students. This building, like many in the area, had two stories, with all of the units facing the parking area in front. It was eleven-thirty PM and the lot was dark and quiet. Nobody would look twice at two guys casually leaning on a truck. J.P. lit a cigarette and laid out the plan.

"She lives alone and hasn't been out since she got back from some kind of meeting about nine o'clock. Her place is on the bottom floor of the building one street over. Her door faces the other side of this one," J.P. reported indicating the apartment building they now stood in front of. "I got two guys and one of their girls. We can use the girl to get her to open the door. Once we get in, it's easy."

Jimbo wasn't nervous exactly, but this had to both go well and be effective. It wouldn't do The Tyros any good if they got away with it, but she didn't quit the election.

"OK, do it fast, but be sure she gets the message."

J.P. smiled. "Oh yeah, dude. Y'all's message will be delivered. I'll call you when it's done and we're out of town."

They shook hands in case anyone happened to be watching. J.P. walked south and disappeared around the side of the building. Jimbo absently checked his phone, mostly for show, and walked away in the opposite direction. But since he was instructed to "supervise" this thing, he turned left at the next block. At the corner, he found he could look around the side of the building and see the entire front side of O'Dell's complex.

TWELVE

Mary O'Dell was tired and having trouble concentrating on her Spanish 410 assignment. She had been at a campaign meeting ever since getting out of class at four o'clock that afternoon and she didn't get home until close to nine. *Maybe it was time for a break.*

Mary lived alone in a one-bedroom apartment furnished with items her family would have otherwise donated to charity. The walls were painted cinder block. The only door opened directly into the main room. There was one window next to the entry door with a loud and inefficient air-conditioner/heating through-wall unit underneath, like those used in motels. A thin wall separated the bedroom and bathroom from the tiny kitchen and living area. The single window in the bedroom provided a view of the blank brick wall across the alley.

Mary was in her favorite spot, curled up on the end of a huge faux leather tan couch. Her parents claimed the couch came directly out of her Grandfather's office when he was president of a small bank in Selma. Mary had no problem believing this. It was definitely from the sixties, maybe even the fifties, and its thick fake leather would probably never wear out.

Mary was stretching her arms over her head and yawning luxuriously when a soft knock at her door startled her. She looked at the clock—11:35. Puzzled because she usually didn't have anyone come by and because she didn't know her neighbors that well at all, she got up, walked over, and asked who was there through the door.

"It's Gina. I live upstairs and I'm real sorry to bother you, but uh, I knew a girl lived here and I well, was wondering if you might have a pad or something I could borrow?"

Mary looked through the peephole in the door and saw the distorted image of a short anxious looking blonde. Mary had a soft heart and she certainly understood Gina's predicament.

"Yeah, sure. Hold on a second," Mary answered.

Mary grabbed a pad and a few tampons from her bathroom and went back to the door. There was no chain, so she had to unlock the deadbolt and open the door. The girl wasn't there! Just as Mary realized this, two huge men pushed her back into her apartment. Her shock and surprise kept her from screaming. By the time her brain realized what was happening, a gloved hand tightly covered her mouth and strong arms pinned her hands behind her back.

Dog and Dog's cousin, Mikey, were first through the door and quickly subdued Mary. J.P. followed behind, quietly closing and re-locking the door. The mini blinds on the window were already shut. All three men wore black sweatshirts to cover their arm tattoos, jeans, and full-face black ski masks.

While Dog held Mary tightly from behind, Mikey removed seven inches of black duct tape that he had previously stuck to the outside of his jeans and taped over Mary's mouth. Dog spun her around and Mikey taped her hands behind her back with a second and longer piece of tape. Neither spoke a word. The three intruders moved so quickly, Mary didn't have a chance, until this moment, to be scared. Now fear washed her like a tidal wave.

J.P. gestured for them to take Mary into the bedroom. Mikey and Dog lifted Mary roughly off her feet and half drug, half carried her into the bedroom throwing her onto the bed face up.

Mary's wide and unblinking eyes stared up at her attackers. Her chest heaved, trying to breath through her nose, her body demanding extra oxygen. She was obviously panicked beyond the capacity for rational thought.

J.P. stepped over to the bed. "Mary," he said calmly, grabbing her face between his hands and placing his face down close to hers. "Mary, look at me. We are not going to hurt you. I need you to listen." Mary tried to shake her head from side to side and began kicking her legs, still uncontrollably terrified. Dog jumped on the bed, straddled her legs and held her down by her hips. Mary futilely thrashed and writhed, quickly becoming exhausted.

J.P. slapped her. "Mary. Look at me," he said again. "Stop." He raised his hand again. Mary understood and finally looked J.P. in the eye.

"We're not going to hurt you," J.P. said. "But listen. Are you listening?"

Mary nodded.

"You have to get out of the election. Do you understand me? Withdraw from the election for president. Get it? Get it?"

Mary's brow furled. *What was he trying to say?*

"Get out of the election or we'll be back, and next time I won't be this nice. Do you understand? You will get hurt and your family will get hurt. Your dad, Warren, mom, Judy, and little sister, what's her name? Oh yeah, Kim. Understand now?" Rick's tone was now deadly serious.

At the mention of her family, Mary's mind engaged fully. She understood and nodded.

"Do it tomorrow and come up with a good excuse. If you tell what happened here, well, I don't want to come back here or take a trip to goddamn Selma to ask your family why you were so stubborn. Got it?"

Mary nodded again. Then tried to scream.

J.P. didn't understand why she had panicked again until he looked back and saw Dog yanking at Mary's shorts. Incensed, J.P. backhanded Dog across the face.

"Fuck man, what the fuck?" Dog cried.

"Get out of here," J.P. ordered.

"Yeah, OK." Dog said disappointed. But he obeyed J.P.'s order and climbed off Mary's legs. "I'll be right outside in case you change your mind."

J.P. looked back at Mary, releasing his grip on her face. "We're leaving. Do what you're told and this will be the last time you see us. Take my advice. You don't want to see me again, ever. Do you agree? Nod."

Mary did.

With that, J.P. stood and left the bedroom, finding Mikey watching out the front window.

"We're good to go," Mikey reported. They all removed their masks and sweat shirts and put them in a backpack J.P. had dropped when first he came in. They walked normally out of the apartment, across the parking lot and down the block, away from where Jimbo had been watching. Dog got in an old Honda with the girl who had called herself Gina. J.P. and Mikey got in Mikey's truck. The groups took separate routes out of town.

Jimbo was impressed. He had seen "Gina" knock on the door, wait for it to open, and just walk away. The moment the door cracked open, J.P.'s team moved smoothly inside with the precision of a SWAT takedown team. After that, he heard no noise at all. No screams, nothing. Minutes later, three casually dressed guys walked out again and disappeared.

"Now that was slick as a willy," Jimbo said to himself. He hoped it worked. This may have been Hunter's idea, but he had pulled it off! He was pleased with himself at the moment, quite pleased indeed.

Mary withdrew from the race the next day.

THIRTEEN

"What's the difference?" Michael King asked Zach on Monday afternoon after Mary O'Dell dropped out of the SGA election. The two buddies sat out on the front porch of the frat house enjoying the warm afternoon sun, having completed their last classes for the day.

"Are you serious? We're unopposed for president! That's the difference. The Tyros is a lock now for the top spot." Zach was incredulous. He couldn't believe his best friend could be so uninterested, even apathetic about the elections.

"That's great. But The Tyros was going to win anyway. It always wins, doesn't it? So, yeah, what's the big deal?" Michael repeated.

"The Tyros doesn't always win dumb butt. Most of the time, sure. But in the past few years, more and more non-Tyros people have been working their way in. For each one of those, there's one less Tyros officer or representative. And, they always make it harder for us to get things our way. You like our seats at the games? You like being left alone by the university P.D.? That's the difference," Zach pronounced.

"Plus, Zach gets a seat at the big table, right buddy?" Michael slapped Zach playfully on the back. "Hey man, I play by the rules. Straight Tyros voting for me, that's for sure. And, I suppose I'll even vote for you since I have to and all." Michael kidded.

"Gee, thanks a lot! I've only known you since the sixth grade," Zach laughed.

"Well how about buying my vote with a beer?" Michael replied. "I'm still sittin' on the fence."

"Drink your own beer. Stephanie's coming over and you know that girl can drink a beer." Zach answered.

"True. I always liked that about her. How long have you two been hanging out?" Michael asked.

"About six months I guess. She may be a keeper. Blonde, beautiful, and a majorette. Oh geez, that sequined outfit! I just love that thing!" Zach sighed, "Life is good."

"You sir, are a lucky man. I can't figure out what it is these chicks see in you. It ain't your looks. That's for sure."

Zach did have a way with the opposite sex. He exuded confidence, never doubting that he deserved the best-looking girls. But that was just Zach, certain everyone he met liked him.

Michael lacked that level of confidence and had always been just a little jealous of Zach's prowess, luck, charisma, or whatever it was. Michael had been dating the same girl now for three years. She was a PTO sister. In fact, Michael might not have come to Alabama at all except for the fact that Sarah was determined to come here and be a part of the number one sorority on campus.

"You haven't done so bad," Zach said. "Sarah's a great girl and you know it. Better than you deserve, that's perfectly obvious. Where is she anyway?"

"Over at the house doing some kind of work for their candidate. I don't remember who it is. You know Sarah, she's as deeply involved as you are. Always into everything."

Michael and Sarah met at their church youth group when they were in eleventh grade. Except for a short and rather stupid breakup because Michael wanted to play the field for a while, they had been dating continuously ever since.

Sarah was a petite brunette, more cute than beautiful. She had a playful nature, but could become deadly serious when focused on a goal. She received a bid to PTO, not because of family connections or money, but because she had worked so hard before and during rush to convince the members she would be indispensible. And she succeeded brilliantly. When time came for PTO to give out bids, Sarah's name nearly topped the list because of her outstanding ambition, loyalty, and spunk. Sarah had thrown herself into sorority life and she was the driving force of PTO's campaign efforts for Tyros candidates.

Michael was Sarah's counterpoint. He saw his job as making sure Sarah didn't get too serious about the whole college thing. Thankfully, Sarah hadn't lost her ability to have fun – not at all. Sarah, on the other hand, kept Michael on the straight and narrow. She made sure he took school and his fraternity seriously. They were good for each other, and they knew it. Their bond was stronger than ever, even after over a year in college.

"So, what are you and Stephanie going to do?" Michael asked.

"My master plan is to hang out here, drink a few beers, see what happens around the house, and then let nature take its course."

"No campaigning tonight? I thought you were going to talk with some club or another. You blowing that off?"

"Nope. I cancelled. When O'Dell dropped out of the race, I guess several other independents lost their will to fight, including the girl running for my place. Michael, as I said before, life is good. I don't even need your vote. You're looking at the next place six representative. The Tyros rules!"

And indeed it did.

FOURTEEN

The Tyros swept the elections in a landslide. It had engineered big wins in the past, but the scope of this election victory was unprecedented. No Tyros candidate lost. A few independents were elected, but only because The Tyros decided not to run a candidate for those positions. Part of The Tyros' overall long-term strategy included leaving several SGA offices without a Tyros candidate. Independent student groups and particularly the campus newspaper, *The Crimson White*, constantly attacked The Tyros during the elections every year. Always on the lookout for a good story, newspaper ran editorials and stories accusing The Tyros of everything from conspiracy to stuffing the ballet box. Staying out of a number of races blunted these attacks and allowed The Tyros to maintain plausible deniability.

Independent students—those not members of fraternities and sororities—outnumbered the Greek population three to one. But only a fraction of Independents participated or voted in SGA elections. The Tyros' power came from the allegiance and dutifulness of its members.

In past elections, a small percentage of non-Tyros candidates collectively received more votes than their Tyros-backed opponent. If several organizations banded together and promoted block voting for an independent candidate, then The Tyros could be beaten, at least occasionally. But not this time.

A united and obedient minority easily overcomes a fractured and apathetic majority.

FIFTEEN

The Doyens asked little of Dr. Dave Knox as the years passed, but kept him tied into their organization and worked behind the scenes to be sure he moved up quickly at Lockheed. Dave's career bloomed rapidly, along with his salary, generously augmented from time to time by The Doyens. Within two years, Lockheed executives tapped him to join the elite Skunk Works team. Dave was well aware that The Doyens had some hand in his meteoric rise through the company, but he also knew that it would not have been possible without his own extraordinary expertise in aerospace sciences. Dave's talent and The Doyen's influence made a potent combination.

Almost ten years after taking a position with Lockheed, Dave began the most interesting and challenging project of his career. Lockheed assigned him permanent status at their Groom Lake facility to aid in the development of the GW-FB1. He began work on the flight control systems, later moving to the gravity wave generator and propulsion unit itself. Despite his multiple oaths of secrecy, documented and signed, Dave kept The Doyens informed of his work and the advances being made at Groom Lake. A few days before his first vacation from Area 51, The Doyens contacted Dave, requesting an immediate meeting. Dave flew to Atlanta, telling his coworkers and superiors that he was going to visit his parents.

A cold rain fell over Atlanta as Dave, now thirty-eight, rode the escalator up to the huge open baggage claim area in the Atlanta airport. He intended to rent a car, drive into downtown and check into his favorite hotel, the Georgian Terrace. He traveled light, as usual, with only his leather laptop case and his silver Rimowa aluminum carry-on. It was getting dark and he wasn't looking forward to fighting Atlanta traffic in the rain. But as it turned out, he didn't have to do the driving after all.

At the top of the escalator, behind the area roped off for those greeting passengers, Dave saw "Dr. Knox" neatly lettered in white on a black cardboard sign. A huge man dressed in a black suit and tie held the sign while scanning the arriving passengers' faces as they appeared on the escalator. Surprised to have someone meeting him, Dave walked over and said, "I'm Dr. David Knox."

"Yes, Dr. Knox," the gentleman responded, having to look down to mentally identify Dave from a photo he had studied earlier. "My employers apologize for rescheduling your meeting with them without informing you ahead of time. But they requested you meet with them this evening at your hotel, if that's convenient. They also said to tell you that an excellent bottle of Bordeaux would be decanted when you arrive. I have a car waiting." He did not introduce himself, but his crew-cut hair, obvious physical fitness, and direct no-nonsense manner gave away his military background. The mention of "Bordeaux" was the authentication code used by The Doyens when communicating with Dr. Dave Knox.

"No problem at all. I don't have any other bags. So, lead the way," Dave agreed.

The driver took Dave's rolling suitcase in hand and moved quickly toward one of the exits. The driver stood over six feet five inches tall and his long strides forced Dave into an intermittent jog just to keep up. The "car," the driver quickly located among several limousines in the VIP parking area, was no car at all. The choice of a monstrous black Hummer H2 surprised Dave, but the opulent interior belied the vehicle's aggressive exterior. Dave settled into a soft black leather captain's chair mounted behind the driver. The comfortable glow of the passenger compartment's soft lighting glinted off crystal glasses and decanters mounted in a mahogany bar within easy reach. Dave relaxed while the driver expertly navigated Atlanta's heavy traffic and confusing downtown street layout.

After arriving at The Georgian Terrace, the driver left Dave with the deferential attendants manning the hotel entrance. Walking through the front doors, the concierge, who introduced himself as Thomas, greeted Dave warmly. Thomas explained that Dave was already checked in, his room was ready, and his bag would be taken directly there. Thomas also informed him his hosts were waiting in a private conference room on the mezzanine level and would like for Dave to join them as soon as he arrived.

Although still in the same sport jacket and jeans he wore on the plane, and feeling a bit disheveled, Dave agreed and followed Thomas. As always, Dave admired the early twentieth-century styling and grandiose marble columns standing around the edges of the round lobby. He followed Thomas up the main stairs to the mezzanine and into a small alcove just off to one side. The concierge knocked on a heavy wood door set into the back wall. Dave had stayed in this hotel at least ten times, but had never noticed this alcove or the door within. Without waiting for a response, Thomas motioned Dave to enter. As he opened the door, Dave also had to part two heavy dark red curtains.

After passing through the curtains, Dave found himself in a dark-paneled room furnished with an impressively large, round Spanish-style table. Twelve richly upholstered armchairs were placed around the table at equal intervals. Wall sconces supplied dim but comfortable lighting to the exclusive club-like setting.

Three gentlemen, including The Doyen he met years earlier in the Sundial restaurant, sat at various positions around the table. Despite the intervening decade and a half, he appeared only slightly older than at their first meeting. Dave didn't recognize the other two men.

"Please come in Dr. Knox. Thank you for coming early. I'm afraid it couldn't be helped," The Doyen said. "Please take a seat," he continued, gesturing to the armchair nearest the entrance.

"My pleasure," Dave said.

"These gentlemen are also Doyens in our movement. This is Governor Johnson Burns of Mississippi and this is Governor G. Hunt Smith of Alabama," The Doyen said. Each governor nodded to Dave in turn.

Governor Burns sat to Dave's right. A large man, Burns was barrel-chested and sported a mane of light brown hair pulled straight back over his head. Governor Smith, seated to Dave's left, was a tall but slight man with a rim of short gray hair surrounding his otherwise bald head. A pair of round glasses sat perched on his hawk-beak nose. Smith projected a harsh, judgmental demeanor, sitting ramrod straight in his seat with hands clasped together on the table in front of him. The popular depiction of Ichabod Crane came to Dave's mind. The Doyen Dave met years ago sat directly across from him between the two governors. Just as before, he did not introduce himself by name.

More curious than concerned, Dave said, "An honor to meet you both."

Burns now spoke up in an impeccable Southern accent. "Dr. Knox, it's indeed an honor to meet you as well. We have been watching your career for some time. Very impressive, to say the least. We appreciate your steadfast loyalty and we hope you have found that appreciation profitable."

"Absolutely," Dave replied.

"Good. Good. I'll get right to the business at hand then. We believe it's time for you to move up in our organization. If you'll indulge me, I'd like to give you some background, a broader understanding, if you will, of who we are."

Dave responded immediately, "Of course, please." The meeting had just taken a very interesting turn.

"Thank you," Burns continued. "As you have been aware for some time, The Doyens represent an influential and critical class of the population that is not only wealthy in its own right, but creates wealth and jobs for our society as a whole. What you haven't been told is that we are all Southerners. That is, we, and our families before us, call the states of the South our home. Our work, as it has been for many decades now, is to maintain our Southern way of life and heritage while protecting what we call The Klass, spelled with a 'K', from degradation or even destruction by the federal government. We call ourselves this as a simple representation of our membership."

"I understand. Please go on," Dave said. Although Dave knew some of this already, he hadn't been aware of the exclusively Southern aspect of "The Klass" as Governor Burns referred to the organization he had joined long ago.

"Thank you kindly. Let me do just that, beginning with a little history, if you'll indulge me. Since the formation of our country, the North and the South have been at loggerheads over many issues. And ever since the War Between the States the federal government has, unerringly, attempted to bend the South to its wishes. As an aside, they have found the South quite difficult to change, and I must say that is due to the efforts of The Klass.

"But I digress. Anyway, after the Civil War, the South continued its struggle against what was then thought of as Northern encroachment, but what we now think of as federal autocracy, or complete dominance by the federal government. Back then, semi-organized groups such as the Klu Klux Klan and the Knights of the White Rose resisted federal efforts to change the South culturally, economically, and politically. The actions of the Klan and others were clumsy, unnecessarily violent, and without leadership. But they did manage to forestall at least some of the changes the federal government would have forced upon us."

Burns paused for a sip of bourbon and then went on. "Later, in the early nineteen-twenties, an Atlanta dentist by the name of William Simmons resurrected the Klan with an entirely new agenda. Simmons hired a man named Clarke, a brilliant publicist, who painted a new picture of the Klan. He portrayed them as stalwart Americans, protecting the white protestant majority from blacks, Jews, Catholics, communists, and the like. Few people today realize the scope of Clarke's success. His rather brilliant plan led to over fifteen *million* Americans joining the Klan and voting Klan candidates into public office. But, while Clarke's plan was sound, its execution was most assuredly not. The Klan's principals became intoxicated with power and turned to political corruption to further their personal aims. Once they stopped following Clarke's strategy, the media of the day—newspapers—exposed the corruption and crushed the Klan under its scrutiny."

Dave had listened patiently, but the mention of the KKK as the progenitor of The Klass made him immediately uncomfortable. The look on his face betrayed his concern.

"Ah," Governor Burns said, noting Knox's changed expression and body language. "I know what you're thinking, but no, The Klass and The Doyens are not the KKK. Definitely *not*. I mentioned that history only because The Klass has as its founding members a group of twelve wealthy Southerners, who were, indeed, past members of the Klan in the nineteen-twenties, as were millions of others. But, after the final demise of the Klan, these men needed a way to protect the South from the growing power of the federal government. Their focus was on the government's intrusion into their lives, wealth, and businesses, not the relatively petty problems of race. Those "founding fathers," if you will, held a meeting in this very room in nineteen-twenty-eight. They invited Edward Young Clarke, the architect of the KKK's social and political success, to help plan the South's future. Clarke actually devised The Klass, and we follow his plan to this very day."

SIXTEEN

The Georgian Terrace Hotel, Atlanta, Georgia, February 29, 1928

With the Great Depression looming unseen just over the horizon, twelve immensely rich and influential Southerners met at the Georgian Terrace Hotel in downtown Atlanta. These men owned the iron and steel plants and shipyards, harvested vast expanses of timber, and farmed great swaths of cotton, soybean, and peanuts. Others operated shipping ports, newspapers, and hospitals. Seated in high-backed leather chairs at a beautifully exotic round Spanish-style table, each man maintained equal status. They gathered to discuss their future and the future of the South. The subdued lighting from electrically powered wall sconces matched the group's dim predictions of the future. Several foresaw the rising dominance of the federal government over the states and others feared that would lead to integration being forced on Southern society. They all feared loss of political and economic power. This group chose no name, because it did not exist. The force that bound them together was mutuality of purpose—protect their riches, power, and class.

These gentlemen had invited a special guest for the evening, Edward Young Clarke. Clarke had masterminded the Klu Klux Klan's popular message earlier in the decade, which lifted the Klan out of the realm of obscurity into political and cultural dominance. Clarke's value to this group of men, and their entire class, was his unequaled ability to manipulate public opinion. Like a potter shapes clay by spinning it on a wheel, Clarke molded public opinion into any shape he desired by spinning facts. But these men did not seek publicity; they only sought a schematic for the future, a way to maintain their class as the dominant force in the South.

Several months before this night, they sent Clarke an anonymous invitation to The Georgian Terrace Hotel for this very date and time. The invitation, delivered by a small black boy, left no doubt his attendance was both mandatory and necessary. It read:

> *Dear Sir,*
>
> *Your attendance is hereby requested at The Georgian Terrace Hotel, Atlanta, Georgia, on the 29th day of the month next at 7:30 in the evening. We are in need of your counsel and wisdom on a matter of immense importance concerning the future of a certain area of the country and particular class of persons residing therein. Your expenses shall be reimbursed in full, along with a generous honorarium, at the conclusion of the evening. Please do not consider refusing this invitation. Past associates of yours, whom possess considerable relevant skill, are charged with ensuring your safe attendance or punishing the opposite with vigor.*

Please present yourself to the Concierge upon your arrival.

The invitation was signed with a single small red cross.

Precisely at 7:30 in the evening on the twenty-ninth day of February 1928, Clarke nervously entered The Georgian Terrance Hotel and crossed the impressive circular lobby to the concierge desk. The attendant greeted him warmly, relieving Clarke's stress a small degree, and led him up the main stairway to the mezzanine. Turning left, they entered a small alcove, where the concierge placed a blindfold on Clarke, apologizing for the need for such inconvenience, but explaining that Mr. Clarke's hosts insisted upon complete anonymity. He then led Clarke by the arm through a heavily curtained entry and seated him in a comfortable leather chair. The concierge excused himself immediately. Sitting in awkward silence and with pungent cigar smoke filling his nostrils, Clarke's anxiety returned in earnest.

A man to Clarke's right finally spoke. "Mr. Clarke, thank you for coming. I must apologize for our inexcusably rude invitation. You are seated at a table with me and several utha gentlemen. On the table before you is a tumbala of Kentucky's finest bourbon. Please put yourself at ease as you are in no dane-ga. We are in need of your sage advice, so you are quite safe."

The person speaking was obviously Southern, and Clarke concluded from Georgia. They needed his advice? Now more interested than frightened, Clarke called on his skill as a talented publicist and asked, trying to portray casual confidence, "I am obviously at your disposal, so how may I be of service?"

"It's really quite simple, ya see," said the same voice. "We need you to tell us what the fewcha holds for the South, and how the South can rise again."

Edward Clarke's eyes remained in the dark, but his mind saw the bright light of the future. He came to this room frightened, even terrified of what awaited him. But with the simple statement "how the South can rise again," his fear disappeared, vanquished by his dominant personal characteristic—greed. These men obviously needed a plan, a path of steps, in order to reach some ultimate goal. He didn't care a whit about what the objective might actually be. Clarke's instinctive ability to discern people's most deeply seated desires told him he had found a golden goose. If he wished to exploit this opportunity, he had to be bold, but canny, starting right now.

"Gentlemen," Clarke began. "I presume there are no ladies in the room. I can only guess at your final objective. But if I'm not mistaken, and may be so forward, you look to control the states of the South, independent from their current political, economic, and social conflicts and entanglements." When nobody uttered a word, Clarke continued. "I take your silence as at least

tacit acceptance of my proposition. Now, there are many possible reasons for these objectives. Please forgive any presumption on my part, but as I am completely ignorant of your identities, I shall speak freely."

Except for someone tinkling ice in a glass, the room remained silent.

Clearing his voice and summoning his courage, Clarke said, "The South has always maintained its own character and way of life. While there are variances among your states, this way of life is basically consistent throughout the region. You look for it to remain so in the future."

After waiting a beat and again receiving no response, Clarke ventured on. "The center of Southern society has always been the upper classes, those families whose hard work and ambition earned them just rewards. Wealth gained by those efforts, over many generations, has inevitably and correctly led to political prowess and thus significant control." Clarke decided this bit of flattery would strike the right chord. Then he said, "After the War Between the States, the upper class's influence diminished significantly and still, today, lies at a very low ebb indeed.

"Finally, I surmise that your reason for exploring this, uh, future vision, is the continuing and increasingly shrewd incursion of Washington, D.C. into your lives. The government of the United States of America now imposes not only its morals, but also its unfettered will over the states. I dare say that you gentlemen are concerned, and

rightfully so, that you and your entire class will be forced to relinquish the freedom, social position, and political influence earned through honest struggle over the past one hundred and fifty years."

Now Clarke set the hook. *"I apologize again if I have presumed too much with the little information I have at hand. However, if I have correctly analyzed your situation, or even come close, I may indeed be able to offer some suggestions."*

The twelve men around the table paid rapt attention to Clarke as he spoke. While they were awestruck by his quick analysis and accurate conclusions, they now had to decide whether to entrust Clarke with their identities and listen to his advice. One by one, each man around the table nodded at the only man whose voice Clarke had yet heard.

"Mr. Clarke, we are impressed. You are fundamentally correct in your analysis. In fact, you are exactly on point," the chosen speaker said. *"But our reason for bringing you here wasn't to have you deduce our goal or describe our reasoning. We brought you here tonight for advice on how to proceed."*

Clarke's plan worked! By first enticing them with nothing more than simple deductions from the *"invitation"* and what he was told verbally, Clarke could keep doling out very expensive advice for a long time to come.

Clarke replied, *"I understand your request. But, if you do indeed want an effective and ultimately successful course for the future, I will need to know you gentlemen personally. Any planning must be tailored to both the needs of your particular businesses, locales, and circumstances and to all the capabilities that can be called upon within your class. Second, I will need access to your states' political apparatus to formulate a coherent platform. Finally, a generous salary for myself would not be out of order. With all humility, it was I that found a way to bring the Klan out of obscurity and into the reality of political prominence in just a few years. And it was my message, carefully created and implemented, that gained the Klan the support of millions."*

Clarke waited. He knew his bold demands would either further impress these men, or enrage them. If it was the latter, he was as good as dead.

After a few moments, the first speaker called out, "Mister Concierge!"

Just seconds later, the same man who led Clarke into the room reappeared. "Yes, Sir?" he said.

"Please take our guest to the seating area and arrange a drink for him. I shall call you again shortly."

Without a word, the Concierge once again took Clarke politely by the arm and led him out of the room. Once outside, Clarke removed the blindfold, blinking at the bright electric lights from the chandeliers above. Relieved to be out of the stuffy, smoke-filled room, Clarke ordered a glass of champagne. He normally drank whiskey, but right now he needed something refreshing. Using his time wisely, Clarke devised the basic strategic framework that should fit this group's ambitions and keep him employed indefinitely.

Thirty minutes later, the concierge approached Clarke, informing him he had been asked to return to the meeting. This time, no attempt was made to blindfold him—a promising sign.

The concierge led him back to the entry alcove and simply pulled back the heavy curtain, gesturing with a white-gloved hand for Clarke to enter. As Clarke moved through the entrance, he counted twelve men seated at a round table. As his eyes adjusted back to the dim lighting, Clarke realized he knew these men—all of them. Nearly the entire upper echelon of the old Klu Klux Klan from North Carolina to Texas sat before him!

"Very impressive, Mr. Clarke." Gerald A. Reeves, the owner of half of the buildings in Atlanta and several other cities, said. Reeves had been the group's earlier spokesman. Reeves stood, reached out, and pumping Clarke's hand went on. "Very impressive indeed! We needed to be sure of your, uh, continued interest, before bringing you back. We have agreed that all of your requests will be met. Now, if you would, sit down and indulge us with a bit of foresight. What do you see as a first step?"

Confidently and seriously, Clarke looked around the room. Once he had the attention of every man there, Clarke said, "Gentlemen, Mr. Reeves himself has pointed to your initial challenge. Your first step is to develop foresight. The Klan is dead. It is a thing of the past that is of no further use and must not *be resurrected. Look to the future. Your aims cannot be attained this year or the next, in this decade or the next, or be attained by your generation or the next. Your first task will be to realize that simple fact and plan accordingly. Patience is the key. Your second step shall be to develop leaders of what I'll call "The Klass." Your class. Please forgive my nostalgia if I spell "Klass" with a "K." These leaders shall be called The Doyens, an ancient word for a "leader" and "teacher" combined. They should be chosen for their intelligence, talent, wealth, and influence. The Doyens you choose must themselves choose and instruct the next generation of Doyens and so forth. The Doyens will carry the plan forward from one generation to the next. Keep The Klass strong, organized, and beyond all else, secret. To this basic framework we can add the flesh of a fully developed plan of action. Once fully formed and prepared, The Klass can achieve the independence and security it deserves.*

SEVENTEEN

After finishing his history lesson, Governor Burns settled back in his seat. "You see," he said, "y'all are part of a movement with a long history. My own great-granddaddy sat at this table. My grandfather and father sat at this table and I am here today. Governor Smith's family was invited here before the end of the Second World War."

"I'm certainly impressed, but not surprised," Dave Knox stated truthfully, reassured that his benefactors were not some reincarnation of the KKK. "The gentleman at the end of the table alluded to something like that years ago when we first met, and I've surmised at least some of the rest. The Klass has always treated me well and I've strived to be worthy of its confidence and trust. I hope to so continue."

"Ah," the unidentified gentleman said from the other side of the table. "As I expected, you've hit upon the heart of the matter. Yes, you have indeed proved yourself, time and again. Now we'd like you to take on an assignment with authority to act as you see fit."

Dave voiced his curiosity and interest. "I'm intrigued."

The Doyen responded, "Excellent. You have kept us informed of the research being done using gravity waves. We see this as nothing less than a game changer in the defense industry. To be frank, we want it. And, we want to have exclusive use of it. You are in a unique position to accomplish obtaining it for us. The Klass has been waiting for decades for a breakthrough that would afford us unprecedented and near absolute defensive capability. As we understand it, this GW-one aircraft can provide such an advantage."

"Am I to understand you contemplate some kind of military action? And if so, against whom?" Dave said with apprehension in his voice. "I'm afraid I don't understand."

"To answer your question directly," The Doyen responded, "absolutely not. Our need for the technology rests in the avoidance of any kind of conflict. We see this as a chance to free ourselves from any threats once our overall plan is implemented."

"Look," Dave replied. "I've kept you abreast of developments in my work, which would certainly get me fired or perhaps even arrested. But what you're asking me to do now is an act of treason. In fact, considering, even briefly, how I might undertake what you're suggesting presents me with no option where I'm not ultimately identified and labeled as a traitor. I don't relish the thought of being hunted by every law enforcement agency in the country for the rest of my life; which would likely be quite short."

The Doyen could understand Dave's hesitation, but on the other hand, Dave had not yet absolutely refused the assignment. He needed this man to believe in the absolute necessity of this action and that he would be protected after it was accomplished. He decided to tap into Dave's ambitious nature and reveal as much as he needed to know about the definitive objective of The Klass.

Now deadly serious, the unidentified Doyen responded, "Your questions and concerns are absolutely understandable. When we said you were to be given more responsibility, we were referring not only to the responsibility of this task but of deepened knowledge of the ultimate aim of The Klass. With this knowledge, you will pass into the upper echelon. This moment marks a turning point in your life, but you must grasp this opportunity now; or you must turn it down. What do you say?"

The affect on Dave was profound. *A treasure chest had just been opened!* Avarice glinted in his eyes. His answer came in a rush that he didn't intend. "I say yes! Oh hell yes! I most certainly accept. Please, go on."

The Doyen did so. "You grew up in the South, but have spent considerable time in other parts of the country. I expect you have found that we Southerners are quite unique. Our way of life and beliefs run deeply through our veins. We don't and never have seen eye to eye with the rest of the country.

"The South's distinctiveness rests in our idea of freedom. We believe that freedom doesn't mean that we are free to travel from one state to another, free to choose what we eat for dinner or free to choose the car we drive.

True freedom, to us, means total freedom from government interference in any aspect of our lives. To act as we see fit. Government should be only what the people say it should be and no more. In our view, the rest of the country has voluntarily given up its rights in exchange for the government's unsustainable promise to take care of them forever. And, we believe the federal government is trying to take what remains of our rights as Southerners without our consent. We are spied upon in our own homes, our telephones bugged, our movements tracked, our computers scrutinized, our guns registered, our businesses regulated and our markets manipulated. Our forefathers bought freedom for this country with their lives in the seventeen hundreds. And they challenged the government's usurpation of their rights less than a century later. Freedom, once earned, must be protected. That is why we want the GW-one, to protect and assert that freedom."

"I get what you're saying," Dave said looking at the table and thinking out loud. "I agree one hundred percent, but how does gravity wave technology and the GW-one meet that end? In and of itself, it cannot …."

Dave looked up.

"Oh my God."

EIGHTEEN

After that night, Dave's commitment to The Klass filled his entire existence. The Doyens' revelation transformed him. Dr. David Knox now saw himself as much more than just a member of an elite organization and a talented scientist. He was a patriot.

Returning to Area 51, Dave set his massive intellect to the business of providing The Klass with exclusive possession of gravity wave propulsion. However, exclusivity would be problematic. The majority of the technological development had already taken place and could be easily recreated. He needed to "acquire" an integral part of the system, before it could be finalized. Dave set himself the task of scrutinizing each system of the GW-FB1 separately for any opportunity. His mind fell upon one indispensible part of the system still delaying full operational status—the fuel for the gravity wave reactor.

Element 128, the super-heavy, artificially manufactured element necessary to power the reactor, had only recently been discovered. Despite significant research, Element 128 could only be created in small quantities by sophisticated and time intensive manipulation of raw materials in a laboratory. Like driving a car with only a cup of gasoline, the GW-FB1 prototype could fly for only about five minutes, simply because Element 128 wasn't available in sufficient quantity. Before the GW-FB1 could be deployed, the Skunk Works needed to invent a process to manufacture Element 128 in quantity. To date, the solution to this problem had eluded the best minds of the GW-FB1 team.

With his target technology identified, Dave used his seniority and natural persuasive ability to be appointed lead scientist of the Element 128 manufacturing process effort. Dave's team initially met with little success. However, after first recruiting Rick Donnelly to the Skunk Works and eventually on to his Element 128 processing team, the answer came quickly. Rick had the unique ability to create solutions to problems nobody else could solve. Dave then engineered the actual nuts and bolts instruments and devices needed to implement Rick's processing solution.

During their close collaboration, Knox became convinced that Rick's talents would be imperative, even after he placed the key to continuous gravity wave generation into the hands of The Klass. So Dave began meticulous efforts to recruit him. As Dave got to know Rick at Area 51, he discovered Rick's political beliefs were, if not radical, certainly compatible to Dave's covert assignment. Rick's thirst for friendship made him easy to sway and Dave took advantage of the fact that a person like Rick with delicate self-esteem and no social life relishes joining a welcoming organization.

Dave slowly convinced Rick of the absurdity of the military having sole access to gravity wave technology. Further, the government's ironclad control over the project stifled its development. Rick came to believe that private citizens, who had paid for it in the first place, could better utilize this breakthrough in power. Rick eventually accepted Dave's promise that his associates would allow gravity wave technology to reach its fullest potential. But, Rick maintained strong objections to taking highly classified information, even for the sake of true scientific advancement.

Dave found himself in a dilemma. He undoubtedly needed Rick's help, but to get it, he needed to up the ante. Without seeking further authority from The Doyens, Dave revealed The Klass and its objective to Rick. The guarantee of freedom from government's domination of scientific development did the trick.

Anyone can be motivated to commit extraordinary acts if given the right reason. Rick's motivation for committing treason turned out to be Dave's promise of unfettered scientific research guaranteed by The Klass. Dave Knox's flair for reading and manipulating people rarely shone more brightly. Now they needed a plan of action.

Both Dave and Rick had been the subject of comprehensive background checks and vetting by several government agencies. The FBI, NSA, and the intelligence arm of the Air Force all checked and re-checked every aspect of their lives. To be a part of the Skunk Works team meant the employees, by definition, had to be both trustworthy and trusted. Incredible advances could not be achieved without giving the brilliant minds involved freedom to think creatively, consult with outside colleagues, and work closely with each other. Dave and Rick formed an ingenious method of slowly and methodically transferring small but integral parts of the gravity wave project and GW-FB1 specs to their own computers. They found taking often-indispensible information no more complex than claiming they needed it on their laptop for further study or emailing "colleagues" small pieces of information for consultation. Dave took charge of the operation, making certain Rick didn't overstep security boundaries or get cold feet.

Air Force Intelligence officially logged and approved each transfer of data. Lockheed security personnel suspected nothing. And, Dave's end game would assure it didn't matter anyway.

NINETEEN

The morning after his first meeting with Rick Donnelly in Birmingham, Drew Campbell placed Rick's package in his safe. He also opened a new file under the client name "R. Donnelly" for billing purposes. Of course, Tracy, his excitable assistant, was almost obscenely curious about the mysterious new client. Trying to avoid a lengthy explanation, Drew just said that Mr. Donnelly was just a friend of his who might want to open a business. It didn't work. Tracy knew Drew deposited $25,000 in the firm's trust account, and that *never* happened.

Drew didn't hear anything at all from his new client for the next two weeks. Any lingering expectations or apprehensions about representing Rick dissolved away as the time passed. Drew felt certain Rick would get in touch with him when he wanted to move forward with his business project. Nobody hands over twenty-five grand and then just walks away. But Drew's caseload had recently spiked and he thought little about Rick and his package of documents. But that was about to change.

At 1:30 in the afternoon, two weeks to the day after meeting Rick, Drew was just finishing his usual turkey sandwich and relaxing at his desk with a book. Drew almost always ate at his desk, but he also used the time to put his feet up and relax. He enjoyed adventure novels, or something equally entertaining. He also enjoyed historical biographies and today he was close to finishing the new biography of Harry Truman.

Drew couldn't help but like old Harry. This biography portrayed him as honest and down to earth in a plainspoken, Midwestern way. While Truman was undoubtedly prejudiced and even a one-time member of the Klan, he also integrated the armed forces and recognized the State of Israel immediately upon it declaring itself a sovereign nation. He wasn't the brightest bulb to ever become president, but Drew respected the fact that the man could make a decision.

Just as he put the book aside, Tracy burst into his office through his partially closed door.

"Uh, Drew, it's the FBI!" Tracy announced breathlessly. Drew wondered how she could get out of breath just walking twenty feet down the hall.

"What the hell are you panting about?" Drew asked.

"OK," Tracy gasped. "There's an FBI...agent...want to...see you."

"Right. Did he have a badge and everything?" Drew said with dripping sarcasm. Tracy had a way of getting worked up over almost anything.

"You really should just come up to the front with me!" Tracy said firmly. She had partially caught her breath and was now standing with her hands on her widely spaced hips. Tracy sounded uncharacteristically serious. He figured he better just go see what she was worked up about.

Drew walked reluctantly down the hall to the reception area and stopped behind the counter that separated the waiting area from Tracy's desk. Sure enough, he found a man in a dark suit and tie standing stiffly on the other side.

"I'm Drew Campbell. Can I help you?" Drew's nerves suddenly flared up, but he didn't know why, other than the fact that he had never met an FBI agent. He never really thought he would.

"Mr. Campbell, I'm Special Agent Frank Deal," the agent said, introducing himself. Deal simultaneously produced his credentials by flipping open a small leather wallet revealing a badge and identification card. "May I have a moment of your time?"

"Sure," Drew said after looking at the identification. "Let's step into the conference room." Drew gestured toward the double glass doors on the right side of the reception area.

As Drew followed through the doors he asked if he could get the agent a cup of coffee or water.

"No, thanks. This won't take long."

Agent Franklin Deal had served four tours in Afghanistan and Iraq. As a JAG (Judge Advocate General) investigator with the Army, his assignment was to hunt down chemical and biological weapons makers and detain them as enemy combatants. He also held a law degree from Cornell, but had never entered private practice. While dressed in a simple civilian suit, his military posture and top physical condition were unmistakable.

Despite being a JAG officer, basically one of the Army's lawyers, Deal's job in both Gulf Wars wasn't clean or safe. Traveling with a special unit of WMD hunters, he came into conflict with insurgents and terrorists on many occasions. In fact, he had two Purple Hearts for injuries to his right leg and right shoulder, courtesy of a couple of perturbed locals who didn't like his unit snooping into their business. Deal's unit had returned the courtesy with extreme prejudice. Both attackers died violently.

The FBI recruited Deal after he retired from the Army for his expertise in investigating and locating producers of WMD components. This background made him the perfect choice for the assignment that had brought him to Drew Campbell's office.

Drew indicated one of the conference chairs at the side of the table while he took his usual seat at the end.

"So, what can I do for the FBI?" Drew inquired. He surprised himself with the offhandedness of the question.

"I don't want to waste your time, Mr. Campbell. I work out of the Birmingham office and we've been asked to look into the movements of a certain individual over the past several weeks."

"So, who is the subject of this inquiry?" Drew asked with unusual formality. *It was always best to assume full lawyer-mode when dealing with a new situation.*

Dan Klasing

"Richard Donnelly. Goes by Rick. We believe he was in Birmingham a couple of weeks ago. Not trying to be blunt, but do you know Mr. Donnelly?" Agent Deal had taken a small notebook out of his jacket pocket.

"I do. But I expect you already knew that. We had dinner about two weeks ago. I need to inform you now that Mr. Donnelly hired me as his counsel." *Oh crap*, he thought, *what did Rick get me into?*

"Yes. Of course. We did know that you and Mr. Donnelly met last week. We didn't know that he hired anyone as his counsel." Now it was Agent Deal's turn to be surprised. "May I ask what he hired you to do?"

"Agent, you know that you may certainly ask, but you also know that I can't discuss anything I talked about with my client," Drew answered.

"Can you at least tell me if Mr. Donnelly gave you anything?"

"No," Drew answered. "I'm ethically bound by the attorney-client privilege and I'm afraid that ends our meeting, unless you want to talk about something other than my client." Drew made a move to get up, implying that Deal should as well. But Deal didn't get up. Instead, he sat back in his chair and interlaced his fingers behind his head. He looked at Drew for a long moment, scanning him for any sign of evasiveness.

"Where did you meet Mr. Donnelly?" Deal finally asked. "That's not some kind of privileged information is it?"

Drew sat back down, now becoming irritated. *Apparently, Deal wasn't impressed with his stern-attorney act.*

"I met Mr. Donnelly on a Southwest Airlines flight from Las Vegas to Birmingham. I believe it was early to mid September. I can get the date from my calendar if you need it," Drew offered, although he surmised Deal probably had that information as well.

"No thanks. We have all that," Deal said coolly.

Drew didn't react to Deal's attempt to intimidate him with the FBI's investigative prowess. Drew certainly hoped the FBI could look up flight numbers. Although, thinking about it further, Drew remembered that Southwest Airlines didn't offer assigned seating; so, there would have been no seating chart to follow. Now Drew's mind began to think like a lawyer. How did they know Drew *met* Rick on that flight? Drew quickly realized they didn't, but they had theorized this was the case when they checked up on Drew's movements after they discovered he had dinner with Rick. Deal was just looking for confirmation and he had easily gotten Drew to give it to him.

"Can you tell me what you talked about during the flight? I mean, I assume you weren't his attorney at the time," Deal continued with a hint of sarcasm.

"I can, only because we had no attorney-client relationship. But perhaps I might inquire why my conversation on a random airline flight is so important to the FBI?" Campbell wanted Deal to reveal some reason why he was here.

"National security," Deal replied trying to throw this testy lawyer off his game.

"Not good enough, agent. I don't have to answer any questions unless I want to, so fill me in. Why should I sit here, not billing my clients, having this conversation with you instead? I really don't mind helping you out, but I need more if we are going to continue." Drew stood again.

"OK, OK. Why are lawyers always so difficult?" Deal asked, obviously rhetorically. "We need your help and it is, actually, a matter of national security. Your revelation that Donnelly hired you as his counsel complicates things. But, I'll share the broad strokes with you. Then you can decide what you should do for your client, yourself, and your country."

TWENTY

Drew sat back down. Deal was serious.

"Uh huh," Drew said slowly. "What's this really about?"

Deal leaned back in his chair, ran one hand through his hair, and sighed with resignation. When he sat back up, he leaned forward, placing his forearms on the table, and looked at Drew.

"This is about the most important scientific and military development of the century, if not all time. And, I have authority to tell you about it if necessary. I think it's necessary. I must warn you before I start that this information is classified and we must require you, as a citizen of the United States of America, not to reveal what you hear in this room."

Drew replied with a reluctant nod.

"Before I go further, I have to be sure we aren't being recorded." Deal reached into his coat pocket, retrieving his mobile phone. After running through the options and entering a few numbers, he held the phone over his head for about five seconds. Checking the screen he said, "All good."

Drew didn't know if Deal was really checking for bugs with his phone or just acting like it to get Drew to reveal if he was, in fact, recording the conversation. Apparently finding nothing, Deal replaced the phone in his pocket.

"I'm sure you know of Nicola Tesla, inventor of radio, AC power, and wireless transmission of electricity. Astounding inventions to be sure. But in his later years, Tesla had even bigger ideas. Tesla invented and designed a new type of flying machine."

Drew looked profoundly unimpressed, but remained silent.

"No, not an airplane, which relies on the manipulation of air, but a craft that flies through the manipulation of gravity."

"What? Are you trying to tell me Tesla actually invented a way to defy gravity?" Drew blurted, obviously angered. "That may be the wildest story I've heard in my life! Agent, I don't have time to listen to nonsense."

"Yes, Mr. Campbell, I am saying exactly that," Deal answered firmly. "I know it sounds incredible, but please hear me out."

Drew crossed his arms and sat back in his seat. He would listen, but his bullshit alarm was ringing—loudly.

Deal carried on despite Drew's defensive posture. "When Tesla died in nineteen forty-three, the government took custody of his papers. Tesla's ideas and theories were radical for the time, even unbelievable to most. But, based on his accomplishments, they couldn't take the chance his technical material would become public or fall into enemy hands. World War Two was in full swing at the time of his death, and the Germans already had a big technological lead. The United States needed to catch up.

So, right or wrong, Tesla's work became the property of the United States government.

"Tesla's materials actually jump started America's technical dominance. Work began immediately on his gravity wave propulsion system, among other things. But, despite having Tesla's plans and utilizing the best minds in the country, gravity wave propulsion eluded us. The scientists working on the problem finally came to the realization that they did not have access to a fuel with enough energy potential to power a gravity wave generator.

"To produce the necessary reaction, they needed a new element, one way above the current periodic table— an order of magnitude above one hundred eighteen, the number of the heaviest proven element. Anyway, over the following decades a few scientists came close, but the elements they had been able to create in the range of one hundred fifteen to one hundred eighteen had a half-life of only few seconds. They needed one that was stable, one with a half life of many years, not seconds."

Drew's understanding of the elements was, well, elemental. But he understood that the number of protons and neutrons contained in the nucleus of an atom determined its number. Whatever this was really about, he doubted Agent Deal would or could concoct such an incredible story. Drew couldn't help becoming pulled into the tale.

Deal continued. "Then, five years ago, a team of nuclear chemists at a DARPA laboratory made a breakthrough. They discovered how to produce elements higher than one hundred eighteen. By just pushing forward, creating elements with higher and higher numbers, they discovered that the half-life became longer and longer as well. When they reached one hundred twenty-eight, they had a completely stable new element. The scientist named it Unbioctium in the chemical series Superactinide. Its symbol is UBO. They nicknamed it 'SuperUbo.' We just call it Element one twenty-eight.

"Once we had Element one twenty-eight itself, a process was still needed to produce it in quantity. Four scientists, all physicists or engineers, discovered the process at a highly classified and secure location. With their success, we held the necessary power needed for practical gravity wave propulsion."

Campbell broke in. "This is all very interesting, but what does it have to do with me or my client? I'm afraid I don't understand."

"Please be patient. You need to know the background here," Deal explained. "As you know, most planes are pushed forward by the power of jet engines. Lift is achieved through low pressure generated by wings. Forward motion is needed to pass enough air over the wings to maintain flight. While our best fighters are getting faster and more maneuverable all the time, they're still limited by the need to maintain forward momentum. Helicopters fly on the same principal, the wings are just arranged as rotating blades instead of fixed airfoils.

"Gravity wave propulsion eliminates the need for wings, tails, control surfaces, and engines that produce forward thrust. A gravity wave craft can be of any shape or size and can be made one hundred percent invisible to radar. It can move straight up or down, stop in mid flight, flip, roll, and turn at right angles. Gravity waves are silent, produce no heat signature and the pilots are subjected to no g-forces at all, even during the most severe maneuvers. The manipulation of gravity itself may lead us all the way to interstellar exploration, unlimited free power, perhaps even time travel.

"This is absolute game-changing technology in almost every way imaginable. In just the short run, no existing aircraft or air defense system can defeat a GW craft. Are you getting the picture here?" Deal said, pausing to give Drew a chance to catch up.

Drew had remained expressionless as Deal explained the GW airplane or craft. His thoughts went immediately to the pictures Rick had sent him in the mail. *Was this the gravity wave craft Dean was talking about?*

"Wow," Drew finally said. And, with all the self-control he could muster, he went on. "That's quite a story. But I'm confused, why come here? What are you accusing Mr. Donnelly of? Treason? Espionage?"

Deal looked at Drew and sat back. He let Drew's question hang in the air above the conference room table.

"Let me put it this way: the critical component to gravity wave propulsion is Element one twenty-eight. Four people knew the formula for its production. Two of the four are dead. Murdered. Mr. Donnelly, your client, is one of the remaining two and they are both missing," Deal explained.

"Not to sound trite, but don't you guys write this stuff down somewhere? Surely others can re-produce the process," Drew said trying very hard not to sound sarcastic.

Deal expected this. "Compartmentalization is the key to secrecy. No one person or group has access to every aspect of a project; so any one failure of security isn't catastrophic. This process though, is the key that unlocks all the potential of gravity waves. Think for a moment about this. In just three years during World War Two, The Manhattan Project produced the atomic bomb. Suppose the critical people assigned to the project, such as Robert Oppenheimer, General Leslie Groves, Enrico Ferme, or Edward Teller, all disappeared or died, save one. And, the last one alive provided the process for extracting fissionable uranium two thirty-five from uranium two thirty-eight, the indispensible process needed to build the bomb, to Nazi Germany? *Verstehen Sie*? (Understand?)"

"Ja." Drew knew a little German himself.

TWENTY-ONE

Deal had successfully stunned Drew speechless. *Had this federal agent actually just told him about a top-secret project aimed at defying gravity? A plane, no, aircraft, that flew with no wings and no engine?* He sat as still as a statue, staring past the FBI agent and out the floor length window into the parking lot.

"Mr. Campbell, are you alright?" Deal asked after a minute or two.

Like a man caught daydreaming, Deal's tone of voice jolted Drew out of his reverie.

"Uh, yeah. Yeah, sure. That's just a lot to take in all at once." Drew hesitated a moment or two to pull his thoughts together. Once he had his feet back under him, he asked, "So what do you need from me exactly?"

"Mr. Campbell, you are the only person that's in contact or may be in contact in the future with Dr. Richard Donnelly. As I said before, we need your help. The process for manufacturing stable Element one twenty-eight in quantity is absolutely essential to gravity wave propulsion. Not to sound alarmist, but if Mr. Donnelly turns traitor and sells the process to China, Russia, India, or any country that has modern aerospace technology, America will be wide open to attack."

Deal explained that no defense existed to the GW-FB1. Only another GW-FB1 could hope to defeat an attacking GW-FB1. Even using an equal craft, the attacking GW-FB1 would have to be located first. No technology on the ground, in the air, or even deployed on satellites could successfully locate and track an operational GW-FB1 in flight.

"Along with the obvious military advantage, gravity wave technology has the potential to provide unlimited power. Either we own it, or someone else owns the golden goose. Let's say Mr. Donnelly decides to sell the process to the Arab sheiks for, oh, fifty billion dollars. They would certainly pay that much just to keep it from replacing their oil reserves. In the hands of an unfriendly country, like China, the economic advantage alone would mean we'd have to start eating a lot of noodles and learning to read Mandarin. It's that big, and you just might be the one man who can help save the United States."

Deal had gone too far. Drew became defensive. "I can tell you right now, I'm *not* the man who can save the United States. I'm an insurance lawyer, who may have been in the wrong place at the wrong time. I don't want anything to do with this crap. I don't even know if you're telling me the truth or just spouting the biggest bunch of bull ever conceived by man. You're the FBI for God's sake, and you can't seem to run down one lone scientist? I really don't know him that well, but I can tell you that Rick Donnelly is no super-spy. Geez, the guy looks like the assistant manager of a shoe department. I don't believe for a minute he's some mad scientist traitor."

"Slow down there, Drew," Deal said calmly, needing to bring Drew away from the edge of panic. "Sure, the FBI always gets its man, just like good 'ole J. Edgar Hoover promised. But we aren't clairvoyant and, rumors to the contrary; we don't use psychics or remote viewers. In practically every case we rely on civilians, who never want to get involved, to solve cases. That's all we're talking about here. The game is the same, the stakes are just a lot higher."

Deal wasn't surprised that Drew lost it for a minute or two. He just hit Drew hard in the face with a national security situation far more serious than the Cuban Missile Crisis of October 1962. Whether by direct attack or by economic devastation, the U.S. faced destruction of no less magnitude than as if Kennedy had failed to prevent World War Three.

Drew regained his composure while Deal explained the need for his help. Campbell knew beyond all doubt that he was involved, whether he liked it or not, because he had unwittingly placed himself between the FBI and a possible traitor. Not to mention the fact that his client might be responsible for stealing the biggest secret in U.S. history. For now though, he needed to simplify the situation. Rick hired Drew to be his lawyer, and that's what he needed to get back to.

"I understand, at least the broad strokes, as I believe you described it. But nothing has changed. I'm still Mr. Donnelly's lawyer and I will act accordingly. I'm no criminal defense lawyer and I'm certainly not going to try to be one. I'll need some time to decide what I have to do in that regard. So, for now, this meeting is over."

"Lawyers. Christ," Deal spouted out, but not in an unfriendly manner. Deal needed Drew to cooperate, but pushing this lawyer wouldn't get him anything in return but pushed back. He decided to take a softer approach. "I understand. I never actually practiced, but I have a J.D. myself. So, do your lawyer-thing and then give me a call," Deal said handing Drew his card. "That's got all my information, call my cell first, then the office. Like I said, nothing takes priority over finding and talking to Mr. Donnelly. If he does show up here or calls, please let me know immediately."

"I can't make any promises right now, but I'll think about all this and get back to you," Drew advised as he showed Deal out of the office.

Deal left the office building, got in his car, and drove away. Drew walked a little unsteadily past Tracy's desk and into his office. Tracy had planted herself in his desk chair.

"Oh my God! You look terrible! What happened? Is someone in trouble? Are you in trouble? I've never seen a real FBI agent before. What's going on?" It didn't look like she was going to let up on her questioning.

Drew waived his hand across his body, motioning for her to get the hell out of his chair. "Everything's fine. They're just looking into some old arson and fraud cases and thought I might have been involved in one of them. I wasn't." He looked at the small clock on the bookshelf near his desk. It was after three. "Why don't you leave early today? I'm beat. Talking to the FBI for almost two hours has thrown me off my game. I'm going for a run and then going home." Drew urgently needed Tracy out of his hair. Luckily, nothing in the world, not even a visit from the FBI, was more important to Tracy than getting off early.

"If you say so. Thanks Drew!" She said over her shoulder as she disappeared quickly down the hall.

Drew sat for another half hour at his desk thinking about Rick Donnelly, Agent Deal, and gravity waves— and learning Mandarin. When he finally left, he didn't go for a run. Instead, he went to his favorite wine shop and bought a $50 bottle of Barolo, his favorite red wine from Italy. Then he went home. Lex was about to get a real earful.

TWENTY-TWO

"Sure, sure, I hear what you're saying," Rick Donnelly was speaking as quietly as possible into a disposable mobile phone, while sitting alone at a small table in The Whig restaurant. The Whig offered him anonymity by being one of the most popular and crowded bars in Columbia, South Carolina.

"It's not that I don't trust you. That's not it at all. I think they've come close. If they have, I can't risk leading them to you or our employers." Rick spoke cryptically, just in case.

Dr. Dave Knox, one of the two remaining people on earth who knew the process for Element 128 production called a few moments before because Rick failed to show up at their new lab as planned. Rick explained how he might have been identified in Huntsville, Alabama, several days ago while at a high-power magnet manufacturing company. Rick knew the FBI or some other government agency might be watching manufacturers of high-power magnets that could operate at normal atmospheric temperatures. Only a few such companies produced these highly advanced magnets and Rick feared it would be both logical and simple for the FBI to keep watch on those facilities.

Rick had arrived at the corporate offices of TRS Technologies just as the employees were reporting for work at 8 AM. He waited in the employee parking area until several staff members walked toward the main entrance together. Rick joined the group as if he was just another employee. Once inside the building he stepped away toward the receptionist counter. While Rick possessed extraordinary talent with technology and physics, he ranked below amateur in spy tradecraft.

Rick explained to Dave that he thought he had been spotted leaving the facility. He had noted two cable company vans parked at the buildings across the street as he arrived that morning. But, only one remained when he left two hours later. He had no idea why this particular detail stuck in his mind, but for some reason, it shook him up. On his way to Birmingham to meet Drew Campbell that evening he made several stops along the highway, to see if the cable company van followed him off the exit. Later, he diverted off the interstate, taking Highway 31 South, for the next thirty miles of the trip, just in case. While he noticed nothing unusual, he never lost the gut feeling he was being tailed.

Rick didn't tell Dave Knox about his meeting with Drew Campbell in Birmingham. But after meeting Drew, he exchanged his rented Chevrolet Camaro RS for a more inconspicuous gray Nissan Altima. He then began a multi-state trek over the back roads of Alabama, Georgia, and South Carolina, culminating in Columbia.

Dave listened patiently as Rick described how his grandmother still lived near Columbia and how important it was to him to see her. His grandmother, Ms. Donnelly, developed dementia several years before and Rick had moved her to the nicest skilled nursing facility in the area. He drove by the one-story brick building several times before parking and going inside. He didn't expect his grandmother to recognize him, and he was right. But, he desperately wanted to see her, perhaps for the last time. It took only a few seconds for Rick to lean over and whisper in her ear that he loved her. Other than a soft expression of confusion, she didn't respond. He leaned over once again and whispered, "I'm a patriot. A Southern patriot." He abruptly turned and left, without seeing the whisper of a smile that floated momentarily across Ms. Donnelly's face.

Dave broke off the story. "Rick, listen man, I understand, but don't be a fool. Tell me a location and we'll send people to get you. You'll be here and perfectly safe in just a few hours. Then, we can carry on with our work. This is too big for me alone and we need your help. Heck, *I* need your help." Dave pleaded. "We have a job to do right now, and our bosses are expecting results. How about it?"

"I'm probably clear. I haven't seen a thing for almost two days now, but I need to be sure. I'll call you back in twelve hours." It was close to midnight, and Rick was lying.

"OK, twelve hours. We'll be ready any time. Please, be careful." Dave ended the call.

Donnelly didn't completely believe Dave. He just couldn't help being paranoid. Not only did he think the FBI might still be on his trail, he also knew that Tom

Grant and Phyllis Dodson, the two other scientists in their lab at Area 51, were dead. Murdered, probably to be sure that only he and Dave Knox retained the secret to processing Element 128. He concluded that he had no choice but to question his own value to The Klass. Dave Knox had all the necessary knowledge to create Element 128 despite Dave's declaration otherwise. His reason for meeting with Drew Campbell was this nagging doubt. If The Doyens didn't need him, he was dead. Unless, they also knew Rick might have an ace in the hole, or in this case, in an attorney's office.

TWENTY-THREE

After Knox ended the call to Rick, he turned around and addressed the one other person in the room, the Governor of Texas, Margie Franks.

"I don't know, he sounds scared."

"Shit, you get that fucker to come in now! This has gone on long enough." When Governor Franks got worked up she fired off expletives in full auto. Realizing this attitude wouldn't affect Dave Knox she backed off. "Sorry Doc, didn't mean to fly off the handle at ya'. But we have to convince him it's all right and that we can protect him. What do you think is really goin' on? You know him better than anybody."

Knox sat down on a stool next to a long stainless steel lab table inside Knox's secreted laboratory and manufacturing facility. The Klass built the new lab exclusively for Knox in the basement of the Speedway Garage on the University of Texas campus in Austin. However mundane the garage appeared, the laboratory facilities deep underneath were state of the art. The basement/laboratory connected to the chemical and petroleum engineering (CPE) building by a short utilities access tunnel. The CPE building housed not only any chemicals needed for the Element 128 processing, but also a Cray mainframe supercomputer Knox could tap into as necessary.

"I think he'll come around. He's done a great job so far. I couldn't have gathered the necessary plans and such from Lockheed without his help. He'll call back."

"He better," Franks said looking directly at Knox. "We can't afford one loose screw fuckin' up the whole thing. He's got twelve hours, then we'll haveta run him down like a missin' steer from the herd."

"Geez Margie, you sound just like a hard-ass Texas politician." Knox said smiling at his own sarcasm.

Margie cracked her own grin. "I gotta keep in practice."

TWENTY-FOUR

The used car salesman couldn't believe his luck. *Nobody walks in off the street and pays cash money anymore! This guy didn't even try to get him down off the twenty-five hundred asking price*!

"Yes sir, you're all set," the salesman said, handing Rick the keys to a 1985 Ford Ranger.

Rick got up and headed for the door.

"Mr. Crandle, don't forget your bill of sale!" The salesman held up a single sheet of paper. "You'll need it to get a permanent tag. That temporary one is only good for thirty days."

"Of course, thanks again." Rick said taking the paper and smiling. "Have a good day."

"Already did, sir. Already did," The salesman answered beaming with delight.

Rick needed transportation. He had abandoned the rented Altima near the Columbia airport and taxied to the nearest used car lot. The Ranger was just what he needed; old enough to not require a title transfer and so anonymous nobody would look twice in his direction. He also purchased a new NASCAR cap when he stopped for gas, apparently proclaiming his loyalty to the number 23. Running it over a few times with the Ranger lent it proper character and completed his new persona.

Rick left Columbia about eleven o'clock the morning after his call to Dave Knox. He delayed even considering whether or not to call Dave until he was on the road. His paranoia intact, he decided to head toward Tuscaloosa, Alabama, and pay a visit to his attorney, Drew Campbell. Rick wasn't thinking straight. He had no real plan, and he obsessed on the idea of checking his "safety net." He also wanted Drew's advice. Rick had no friends, except Dave Knox; and at that moment he didn't know if Dave was being straight with him or not. What if Dave had actually murdered Phyllis and Tom? What if Dave wanted to find him just to kill him, too? What if The Doyens wanted him dead? But, what if they actually needed him like they said? Shouldn't he help? *God*, he thought, *what a goddamn mess.*

A couple of hours later, Rick approached Atlanta from the east on I-20. He had been so pre-occupied with his own thoughts he completely forgot about calling Dave. His options were limited. If he didn't call soon, The Klass might take some drastic action, believing he had decided to give himself up to the feds. If he did call, he would have to come up with some story that would pacify Dave and The Doyens a little longer. He needed time to think.

A few minutes later, and after taking a few deep breaths, Rick dialed Dave's number.

"Oh man, I was worried. You were supposed to call hours ago. Are you OK?" Dave sounded genuinely concerned.

"Yeah, no problem. I'm on the road and it just slipped my mind. I'm on my way there now." Rick replied, doing his best to sound natural.

"Driving?" Dave asked. "Where are you coming from? Will you be in town soon?"

"I'm actually near Nashville. I should be there sometime tomorrow. No worries," Rick explained, sounding calmer than he felt.

"How about letting us pick you up in, say, Memphis? We could fly you down here right away on the G-six," Dave suggested. "We need you as soon as possible. I really need your help."

"Nah, I'll drive. Chill out buddy, I'll see you tomorrow. Let me have a little more free time and we'll knock the thing out when I get there."

Dave had been able to put Rick somewhat at ease by sounding normal and genuinely concerned. But, he still wanted to go to Tuscaloosa first and he didn't want Dave to know his real destination. Not yet.

"Well, alright buddy, I'll cover for you until then, but we really need to get moving. Our employers need the product and we're behind. Tomorrow for sure?" Dave asked.

"Absolutely. I'm going to find a good barbeque place and pig out. Ha! Pig out! Get it? I'll be there no later than tomorrow, late afternoon. See you then." Rick hung up. He felt much better. There was no sign of a tail or surveillance since he left Huntsville days ago, and probably not then either. Plus, he realized he missed his friend and the only person that really understood him, Dave Knox. Having his head on straight again, Rick concluded his paranoia wasn't necessary in the first place.

He should have stayed paranoid.

TWENTY-FIVE

The only thing Zach Self loved more than the politics of an election campaign was actually getting elected. Zach had always considered himself leadership material. Whether he actually knew it or not, though, his motivation to lead was mixed. He wanted to be important to the university and his fraternity and he sincerely wanted to make a difference. But he also needed the recognition to stroke his ego.

Michael King saw less and less of Zach as the fall semester reached its midpoint. The SGA kept Michael's best friend busy with everything from meetings with the administration to organizing fan entertainment at home football games. When Michael did hang out with him, Zach tended to monopolize the conversation with his own activities. Sometimes he even offered Michael unsolicited advice, suggesting things Michael could do to be successful. To Zach this meant becoming more popular, but Michael set his own goals and got self-satisfaction from accomplishing them. Unlike Zach, Michael didn't really give a crap what other people thought. Zach never understood Michael's antipathy about being popular. Despite their differences, the two remained as close as brothers.

In mid October the number two ranked Alabama football team played number five LSU in Tuscaloosa. It had been a great game. Alabama won by seven and earned itself a shot at the number one slot. Alabama fans packed the campus to beyond capacity and LSU contributed to the crowd with a huge number of its own fans. While the Alabama faithful loved to party as much as anyone, LSU fans took it to a whole new level. With LSU's close but demoralizing loss, that level bordered on hooliganism. High alcohol consumption on both sides contributed to fights between fans after the game. Just another normal football weekend in the Southeastern Conference.

After the game, current Eta members and alumni filled the fraternity house and lawn. The fraternity provided free drinks and laid out a buffet for every home game. Eta required members wear sport coats and ties to the game and to socialize with alumni afterward. Parents of members, often past brothers of the frat themselves, took the opportunity to visit with old friends and classmates and make valuable connections with other alumni. All the members, alumni, and guests enjoyed the pretense of a sophisticated Southern "lawn party."

Zach and his stunning blonde girlfriend, Stephanie, mingled with the members and alumni. After the game, Stephanie had returned to her sorority house to change out of her majorette outfit and then met Zach at the house. Stephanie wore a crimson sleeveless dress that hugged her figure and flat sandals. Heals would have sunk into the lawn and made her slightly taller than Zach. As they meandered around the crowded front porch, they ran into Zach's father, an alumni of both the university and the fraternity.

George Self enjoyed Alabama games as long as the team won. If they lost, George's already meager sense of humor and level of tolerance disappeared entirely. Zach anticipated his father would be as happy as possible given the outcome of the game, so he decided to make the most of it.

Zach's relationship with his father required a hefty amount of caution on Zach's part. His father's sense of morality did not allow for drunkenness and debauchery. Knowing he would be in town, Zach avoided drinking all day. If George Self thought his son was neglecting his college responsibilities or wasting his hard earned money, even for one minute, he would pull Zach's funding instantly. George Self was as judgmental and unbending as a Southern Baptist deacon.

George allowed himself exactly one bourbon, neat, on game days. He was taking his second sip when Zach appeared with Stephanie on his arm. Zach and Stephanie were drinking Coke.

"Hey Dad, good game today!" Zach said as he walked up. "This is Stephanie Taylor."

George shook his son's hand. "Pleased to meet you, Miss Taylor," George said formally. "Yes, a good game indeed. But too close. Just what were we thinking, running on that last third down? We gave LSU a chance to tie it up. Thank God for our defense."

"I don't know either Dad, but we won. This puts us alone at the top of the Western Division." Changing the subject, Zach said, "Stephanie is a majorette. She's the prettiest one, too."

"Thanks, Zach, you're too sweet," Stephanie said, blushing. "Would it be alright if I stepped inside and got a sandwich? I'm starving."

"Sure, I'll be out here with Dad. Grab me one, too?" Zach asked.

Stephanie smiled. Stepping away she said, "Nice to meet you, Mr. Self!"

George looked at his son. "So how's school? Grades good?"

"Yes, sir," Zach answered. "I'm also busy with the SGA. We have a vote coming up on next semester's budget. I'm on the committee making the initial recommendations. It's a lot of work."

"That's fine. Just so long as you make your grades." George seemed unimpressed with Zach's role in the SGA. In fact, George never seemed impressed with his son as a whole. His father's indifference left a blank space in Zach's life he had never been able to fill. Perhaps the absence of his father's approval is what made him so hungry for appreciation by other people. These stilted conversations were par for the course.

Zach was about to excuse himself on the pretense of going inside to help Stephanie when Bubba, Zach and Michael's huge friend from Greenville, Alabama, half-staggered up to the porch rail. Holding on with one hand to steady himself, Bubba looked up and saw Zach. Breaking out one of his famous smiles, Bubba slurred, "Zach-r-eee! Roll freeckin' Tide! Where's that smokin' hot majorette, I want to give her a big ol' Bubba hug!"

Bubba's tie hung loosely from his neck, one sleeve of his white button-down shirt was torn and his elbow was bleeding. Obviously quite drunk, Bubba let out a long "Woooo!" that turned a number of heads in his direction.

Zach looked down and asked, "Bubba, where's that ugly red coat you were wearing at the game?"

"Some goddamn LSUers became upset at the sight of my bee-u-tee-full crimson coat and attempted to remove it for me. I had to teach 'um some manners, which I done and then some. But then, some po-lice came by and I must have mislaid it during my, ummmm, rush to get here. Where's the bar?"

George Self watched this interaction with a scowl. When Bubba paused he interjected, "Son, why don't you go inside and get yourself a sandwich instead?"

"Hell no!" Bubba responded, "I ain't ruinin' no forty dollar drunk on no two dollar sam-ich—no sir!" Bubba turned, went up the stairs and disappeared into the house.

Zach couldn't help himself, he laughed out loud at Bubba's logic. Turning back to his father, Zach tried to straighten himself up.

"Son," George said seriously, "that boy has problems. Stay away from him. There's good and bad people everywhere. Fraternities included. I met some of the best men I've ever known right here in this house, but also some of the worst. Find the good ones and stick with them. They'll be there for you the rest of your life. The others will gladly take you down to hell with them."

TWENTY-SIX

After leaving Drew Campbell's office, Special Agent Frank Deal drove directly to the federal courthouse located just a half-mile from Drew's office. He pulled into a gated driveway. A hidden device read a signal from his identification card and the steel barred gate opened automatically. Deal parked and entered the building. His team had set up a small but technically sophisticated office in the basement specifically for this operation.

Deal had not told Drew the entire story. Yes, finding Rick Donnelly was his top priority. But, contrary to what he had told Campbell, Deal did not work out of the Birmingham office and his interest in Donnelly's relationship with Campbell was even more important than he led Drew to believe.

While the FBI knew that Donnelly left Las Vegas on the same flight as Campbell to Birmingham, they had not known of Donnelly's relationship to Campbell immediately. Five expert analysts spent hundreds of man-hours tracking the movements of all the passengers and crew of the flight, trying to find some intersection between them and the known movements of Rick Donnelly. The only connection they discovered was Campbell and Donnelly's dinner in Birmingham. Each had used a credit card on the evening of 1 October. After that dinner, Donnelly fell off the grid entirely and that's where his trail went cold.

Deal also withheld the fact that Doctors Grant and Dodson, the two other scientists working on the Element 128 project had been murdered.

Last Labor Day weekend, Dr. Thomas Grant left the Las Vegas airport in his personal vehicle to meet his family at their vacation home on Goose Lake, near Needles, Arizona. Dr. Phyllis Dodson joined him at the invitation of Grant's wife, but they never reached their destination. After being reported missing by Grant's wife later that evening, local law enforcement and military intelligence agents began an urgent search. The scientists' planned route crossed miles of desert, much of it not covered by cellular towers. After two days with no sign of the scientists or their vehicle, the local police called in the FBI. Three more days passed before the bodies of the two brilliant scientists were found in Grant's car, at the bottom of a reservoir over one hundred miles west of their expected route. A couple hiking near the cool clear water of the remote lake spotted Grant's submerged SUV and called the police.

That same weekend, Rick Donnelly and Dave Knox told the Skunk Works offices they would be staying at The Palazzo Hotel in Las Vegas over the holiday. Despite the frantic search for the other two members of the Element 128 team, nobody thought to check on their actual location until the day after Grant and Dodson were reported missing. Even if they had, their efforts would have been futile. Immediately after checking into the hotel, Donnelly caught the non-stop Southwest Airlines flight to Birmingham. Dave Knox simply got in his own car and drove eighteen straight hours to Austin, Texas.

The FBI knew Knox and Donnelly were friends and often spent their free time together, but this fact alone didn't mean Knox was alive or dead. In fact, even the FBI's best investigative teams were utterly clueless concerning Knox. Deal had no choice but to work his one lead, Campbell's relationship to Donnelly, and hope it paid off.

But Deal wasn't about to rely solely on Campbell to contact him if Donnelly surfaced. Deal ordered his team to place listening devices throughout Campbell's office, in his home and in his car. They also maintained twenty-four-hour remote surveillance of Campbell's office with a series of small digital cameras carefully placed to monitor the exterior of the building. Of course, Deal had access to all Campbell's computers and could listen in to all his calls. Deal did not hesitate ordering this deep intrusion into Campbell's life on his own authority despite the dubious legality of his actions. Deal didn't hesitate spying on Campbell without a warrant, firmly convinced the consequences of losing Donnelly outweighed one man's right to privacy.

TWENTY-SEVEN

Lex arrived at home an hour after Drew's visit to the wine shop. Their teenage daughters, ages sixteen and seventeen, had a rehearsal for the big fall musical at school and weren't expected home until after eight o'clock. Lex could sense Drew's stress immediately.

"Hey Hon," she said cheerfully. "I'm glad you're home."

Drew gave a perfunctory smile. "Hey Sweetie. No meetings tonight?"

Drew and Lex met in law school and had been together ever since. While Drew started his own small firm, Lex worked for a large firm in Birmingham that maintained an office in Tuscaloosa. She represented several school districts and this meant she spent many evenings attending board of education meetings. Neither Drew or Lex enjoyed the pressure of practicing law, but they were both respected in their particular specialties and thankful for successful careers.

Drew believed Lex outclassed him intellectually, but he could at least balance the scales by telling himself he had more common sense and ambition. Others often asked if they practiced law together. This made them both laugh. Marriage between lawyers demanded a lot of care not to act like attorneys with each other and they made a deal long ago that they wouldn't be lawyers at home. Thankfully, their practices never intersected, so they rarely had the need to talk about the law or work at home. Tonight would be different.

Drew poured Lex a glass of wine.

"How was your day?" he asked.

"Same as always. Yours?"

"Insane. Really, really nuts." Drew said seriously.

"Gee, I'm sorry about that. What's going on?" Lex asked sitting down on the well-used family room couch.

Drew sat in his equally worn leather recliner and placed his glass down on an end table within easy reach.

"Well," Drew began, "The FBI came to see me today and now I've got a dilemma, a bad dilemma."

"Uh, you're not in trouble are you?" Lex asked, even though she knew he wasn't. Drew could be described as an anally retentive rule follower.

"No, no. It was about a client. Do you remember that guy I told you about, Rick Donnelly? I met him up in Birmingham a few weeks ago?"

"Sure, the airplane guy or whatever. Is he in trouble?" Lex asked.

"I don't know. I can't tell you everything this FBI agent, Deal, told me. But he's looking for Rick and wants my help to find him. He wanted to know all about what Rick and I talked about." This made Lex raise her eyebrows. "Of course I refused. Attorney-client privilege. He didn't like that, but seemed to understand my position." Drew explained.

"I didn't know he hired you," Lex said.

"Yeah, he gave me a retainer and said he would be in touch. I haven't heard from him or seen him since then. He said he just wanted my help maybe opening a business for him, here in Alabama. I've got twenty-five thousand dollars in my trust account, but since I haven't done any work, it's still just sitting there. Now I've got this damn FBI agent sitting in my office, basically asking me to divulge everything he told me. I don't know Rick well enough to really give a rat's ass, but I'm not going to jeopardize my career by making a mistake with this, one way or the other. What do you think?"

"Well," Lex said slowly, "I take it he didn't have a court order compelling you to do anything, did he?"

"He sure didn't mention it if he did. Anyway, you'd think that would have been the first thing out of his pocket."

"I'm no more a criminal lawyer than you are, so the answer is that I don't know. I do know you can't divulge anything privileged without a solid reason, like you think he's about to kill somebody or something like that." Lex thought for a minute and continued. "You said you haven't seen or talked to him since the day he hired you. It seems to me you don't have anything to tell the FBI anyway. If he does show up, give him his money back and send him on his way. Other than the technical fact that you're his lawyer, you don't owe him anything."

As usual, Lex was right. He'd just fire Rick as a client and let the FBI sort out its own mess. *Agent Deal would just have to save the whole blasted country on his own time!*

"You're right!" Drew said sounding relieved. "I don't owe Rick anything but a refund, and I've got nothing to tell the FBI anyway. You're one smart and extremely good-lookin' lawyer sweetie."

"I'll send my bill later," Lex kidded, also relieved to have Drew's mood lighten up.

Agent Frank Deal overheard this entire conversation in real time by means of a laser microphone aimed at the window of the Campbell home by one of his agents positioned down the block. The laser picked up minute vibrations off the window glass and digitally converted them into sound waves. While Deal never completely removed anyone from his list of suspects, Drew hadn't seemed evasive when they talked in his office; and the conversation he had just heard supported his original impression of the man. Drew's comment about his wife being a good lawyer was right on target. But another lawyer? Christ!

TWENTY-EIGHT

The FBI Counterintelligence Unit, often referred to as Unit CI, is tasked with exposing, preventing, and investigating intelligence activities on U.S. soil. Through this elite unit, the FBI works to keep weapons of mass destruction from falling into the wrong hands, proactively gathers information and intelligence, and protects national secrets and assets. It doesn't matter to the FBI whether the spies they pursue come from Russia, China, the Middle East, or Iowa.

Frank Deal led Unit CI's Mobile Fast Response Search Team; known within the agency as "M-Fast." Deployed anywhere in the country within hours, Deal's M-Fast team took immediate control of any case with suspected intelligence activity. M-Fast often operated outside of normal FBI protocol. The national security of the United States depended on preventing spies from procuring intelligence, or running them to ground if they successfully acquired sensitive information. Deal's targets were invariably well trained, well supported, and highly motivated. Their quarry operated in the shadows, without legal constraint. So, M-Fast played by the same rules—none at all. Deal occasionally took some flack from FBI lawyers for his cavalier attitude toward such niceties as warrants and subpoenas, but his outstanding results bought him a lot of forgiveness and substantial leeway to maneuver as he deemed necessary.

The agent in charge of the Las Vegas field office requested M-Fast involvement an hour after he determined the two murdered scientists found in an Arizona lake held top level clearance at Area 51. The murder of the two extremely valuable, but otherwise unknown, scientists could not be dismissed as a random criminal act. Deal's team landed at Las Vegas's McCarron Airport four hours later.

On the flight out, Deal received a briefing on Dodson and Grant's work from DARPA officials. He learned that Doctors Dodson and Grant, and two other scientists, created and perfected a process for producing a complex fuel in quantity for a gravity wave reactor. The unidentified briefer emphasized the full ramifications of losing this process. While Deal couldn't follow the science, or help being singularly awed by the subject matter, his immediate concern centered on whether the murders were, in fact, part of an intelligence operation. Agent Deal didn't have to wait long for an answer. Just thirty minutes later the same DARPA official reported that every computer file and all hard copy notes on the Element 128 process had disappeared. And, the other two scientists working the project could not be contacted or located.

All right then, Deal thought, *this just got interesting.* The two missing members of the Element 128 team might be dead as well; but with no other leads to go on, Agent Deal ordered his team to begin zealous and unrelenting efforts to locate and arrest Dr. Richard Donnelly and Dr. David Knox.

Using the FBI Las Vegas field office as a temporary base of operations, M-Fast began a worldwide manhunt for Donnelly and Knox. A standard search of airline records quickly revealed that Rick Donnelly boarded a plane to Birmingham, Alabama, just hours before Dodson and Grant's murder. Field teams searched Knox's Las Vegas residence, finding nothing of interest, except for the fact that they failed to find Knox's car. A nationwide Level One law enforcement alert for Donnelly and Knox yielded nothing within the next twelve hours. So, Deal's team did what it did best, it got creative.

Deal focused his attention on Donnelly. Knox's trail had grown cold, but by utilizing the vast resources of the government's intelligence gathering apparatus they might be able to pick up Donnelly's trail. Deal's team collected essential data by electronically following every passenger and crewmember on the Las Vegas to Birmingham flight, through cell phone location, credit card use, and social media. Where that wasn't possible, M-Fast dispatched local agents to lay human eyes on several passengers, in one case literally following a seventy-five-year-old widow to church and to the hairdresser.

Once collected, trained analysts pieced together any possible connections between Donnelly's few known movements and anyone on the flight. After hundreds of man-hours, the team finally placed Donnelly and a lawyer

162

from Tuscaloosa in the same restaurant on the same night. Each had used a credit card. Deal needed only simple logic, elementary deduction, and a sprinkling of luck to pick up the first thin thread of evidence leading to Donnelly. Donnelly had used his credit card only one other time, at the Hertz counter in the Birmingham airport. Hertz reported the car missing after Donnelly failed to return it on time. It was still missing.

Once M-Fast connected Donnelly to Drew Campbell, Deal redirected his efforts toward Campbell. After flying directly into Tuscaloosa from Las Vegas on military transport and setting up their base in the federal courthouse, Deal set his team loose. Agents in white vans, displaying the signage of a fictitious cable company, installed high definition and night vision capable cameras on telephone poles surrounding Campbell's office. The one-story red-brick building with floor-to-ceiling windows sat on a busy street near downtown Tuscaloosa. The roof was a simple hip design covered with architectural shingles. An asphalt parking lot, capable of holding ten cars, separated the law office from the building next door. The front door opened onto a short concrete walkway that led to the sidewalk. Campbell's office was newer than most of the buildings on the east edge of Tuscaloosa's downtown. Once a residential neighborhood, most of the area had obviously been re-zoned for light commercial use.

The four cameras allowed clear views of all sides of the office 24 hours a day. Deal's team monitored the exterior of the building for several days to determine the occupant's routine. Nobody was surprised when the members of Drew's firm maintained a mundane ritual of starting work at eight AM. and leaving no later than six-thirty PM., with Campbell usually the last to leave.

After establishing that one Hispanic woman with a small child came to the office on Sunday mornings to clean, the team prepared to enter, search, and wire the premises. Watching from outside wasn't illegal, but entering and bugging the private property of a United States citizen was patently illegal, not to mention unconstitutional, unless one had a warrant. But to get a warrant, Deal had to produce evidence of some probable cause linking Campbell to a federal offense. Since Deal didn't have any probable cause, he didn't waste time and endure the usual headache associated with arguing with a cranky federal judge. It was enough for Deal that he considered his actions justified, the formalities would just have to wait.

TWENTY-NINE

Deal's handpicked infiltration team waited until the next Tuesday night, really Wednesday morning, to make their forced entry into Campbell's building. The two members of Blue team had over-watch. Blue One provided surveillance of the front from a car parked on the street one block west of the building. Blue Two took up position in a plain blue panel van parked one block North of Blue One to watch for threats from the opposite direction. Red team's three members would go in. Voice activated radios kept the teams in continuous communication with each other. White One, Deal, monitored the operation from team headquarters.

The chosen night provided near perfect cover. It was cold for early November, and a light rain kept people inside. Only one house, across the street and two doors down, showed lights in the windows. The buildings on either side of the law firm were completely dark. An old privacy fence behind Campbell's office building separated it from the back of a dentist's office. A lone streetlight a block away cast only a faint orange glow. Deep long shadows fell across the whole area.

Red team stepped casually from Blue Two's van and walked across the street. Passing behind an old house that served as the office for the accounting firm next door, they paused before crossing Campbell's firm's small parking lot.

"Red One, you are clear," Red Team's leader heard in this ear. Red Team's three members quickly moved across the damp parking lot. Even if someone had passed by on the street at that exact moment, they would have missed the three indistinct black silhouettes. The plan entailed picking the back door lock and shutting down any alarm system. When Red One reached the back door, he removed a lock pick set from a covered pocket on his combat-style pants. Just as he was about to insert the first pick he heard, "Red One, hold. You aren't going to believe this." Red One looked back. Red Three was lifting one of the windows.

"Alright, plan deviation, move in through the window," Red One said quietly.

Led by Red Three, they each ducked through the window and Red One closed it softly again behind him. "White One, we're in," Red One reported.

"Acknowledged. Proceed."

"Red Team, switch to night vision," Red One ordered. "Per plan, no lights. This place is like a fish bowl with all these windows. Red Two, alarm check."

Red Two had already pulled a device from her shirt pocket and turned it on. "I read two commercial quality motion sensors. Probably pointed down each hall. Wireless signal to a pad hard wired to the phone. Child's play."

Red Two disappeared out the office door. A loud chirping began, but after less than ten seconds, it abruptly stopped.

"Disarmed. No signal out. We're clear," Red Two reported.

"Alright, let's get it done," said Red One.

Each team member moved swiftly and efficiently. Red Two placed six digital microphones around the office. In Drew Campbell's office, she hid the device inside a wall outlet behind his desk. Several others were similarly placed so that a conversation anywhere in the office could be clearly monitored and recorded. She also opened both of the commercial motion detectors in the halls and installed wireless video cameras.

While Red Two installed surveillance equipment, Red Three located the firm's computer server. With a few strokes, he confirmed that all the computers in the office were backed up to that computer. Inserting a thumb drive, Red Three downloaded the servers' entire contents in less than four minutes. A second thumb drive installed a program that allowed a remote computer to mirror every other computer in the office, constantly uploading every new email message, document, court filing, and male enhancement advertisement. Within less than fifteen minutes, the FBI was in possession of every byte of information that touched the firm's computers and could monitor what each user was doing in real time. A search of the office located no old computers that might contain more information.

In the meantime, Red One searched for locked filing cabinets, locked desk drawers, and safes. *These must be the most trusting lawyers in the whole world,* he thought. Not one desk was locked and the long filing cabinets storing neatly arranged paper files were all open. Thinking they must have some on-site secured storage, he swept the entire office, finally locating a small fireproof safe in a storage closet. Examining it further, Red One determined that this make and model could be purchased at any big box office supply store for less than fifteen hundred bucks. No challenge at all.

"Red One to White One," he said contacting operations command center.

"White One," he heard.

"White One, I need the combination for a Nicholas Safe, I'll read you the number." Red One found the identification number etched on the side of the door and read out the sixteen numbers.

"Stand by."

Red One sat down in front of the safe. After about thirty seconds White One read the combination. The FBI did not have authority to hack into the computers of safe manufacturing companies and appropriate combinations at will; but, since they were already breaking dozens of state and federal laws tonight, cracking one safe wouldn't matter much anyway.

Red One used the combination to successfully open the safe and, after checking that his headlamp could not be seen from outside, turned it on and looked inside. Half the safe was stacked with legal-size brown envelopes. Red One immediately noticed that the top envelope's color differed from those below and appeared to have gone through the mail.

Red One removed the top envelope, turned it over and immediately saw the Pratt & Whiney logo. After carefully opening the envelope and removing the two-inch thick stack of papers stuffed inside, Red One saw that he clearly held the reason for tonight's infiltration in his hands. Red One only had to thumb quickly through the pages to see that he held miniature blueprints for an advanced military aircraft.

"White One, all mission objectives successful. Red Two and Three, time to go," Red One ordered.

THIRTY

Drew drove to work the morning after Agent Deal's visit with Deal's story playing over and over in his head. His mood was foul and his minor hangover from the prior night's wine consumption didn't help. Drew kept coming back to the fact that Rick Donnelly was his client. That simple fact meant something to Drew, but he also felt deep frustration. If what Agent Deal said was true, then Rick had deceived him at the restaurant the night they met in Birmingham. If Rick just hadn't given Drew that package—*that package*! Drew hadn't thought about it for weeks. *Could he be in possession of stolen government documents? What the hell was he going to do about that?* His thoughts remained jumbled as he pulled up to his office.

Drew belonged to a four-man law firm. He and one of his buddies from law school, Doug Hamner, started the firm on a wing and a prayer almost fifteen years ago. Doug was a good guy and a fine lawyer. Drew knew that without Doug he wouldn't have had the guts to leave the large Birmingham firm he had joined right out of law school. But, it was Drew's ideas, ambition, and business sense that created the firm from nothing and kept it going in its first few years. The firm now employed two other lawyers as associates, but only Drew and Doug actually owned the firm. Generally, the two partners of Campbell & Hamner, P.C. made a good team. Drew managed the firm's business and was the brains of the outfit; while Doug was the "front man." Blond and good-looking, Doug was excellent in front of a jury and even better at keeping clients happy with extravagant dinners, trips to Birmingham strip clubs, and junkets to the casinos of Mississippi.

Sometimes though, their diverse styles clashed. Drew followed the rules, conserved the firm's assets, and ran the firm like a captain commands a ship. Doug tended to be more of a free spirit and chaffed at Drew's insistence on very conservative money management.

After walking inside, Drew went straight to the kitchen and poured a cup of black coffee into his favorite mug. The stained and chipped mug still showed a faded picture of his oldest daughter at age three, holding her favorite doll. Drew popped three Advil and hurried to his office. Tracy was nowhere to be seen. *Thank God for small favors,* he thought.

Drew sat down and put both feet up on the corner of his desk. Leaning back, he sipped at the hot brew, letting its warmth calm his nerves. Now settled, Drew once again considered the package in the firm's safe. He hadn't even opened the safe since he put Rick's documents inside weeks ago. The firm only maintained the fireproof safe to hold its important documents and backup media for closed files. Manila envelopes containing life insurance policies, firm corporate documents, and tax returns were simply stacked inside.

Drew didn't tell anyone he put Rick's documents in the safe. It just hadn't occurred to him.

After twenty minutes of sitting quietly and mulling over what he should do, he finally realized he had to make a decision. Right or wrong, he couldn't stand another day under pressure like this. He was over forty and hellish stress like this might kill him.

"Screw it!" he said out loud to nobody. Drew got up and stalked down the hall to the large storage closet where the safe was kept. The safe sat on the floor on the left wall of the walk-in size space. The other walls were lined with shelves holding office supplies of every description. Drew threw open the closet door and knelt by the safe to work the dial of the combination lock. For some reason, Drew rushed turning the dial and missed a number. Cursing under his breath, Drew more carefully entered the combination. This time the mechanism clicked, indicating it was unlocked.

Drew looked back into the hall to see if anyone was watching. Nobody appeared. Turning back to the safe, Drew grabbed the handle and opened the door. Drew remembered what Rick's package looked like. It was thicker than the other envelopes and he had put it right on top of the stack. But he didn't see it! Thinking Doug might have been messing around in the safe, Drew looked again. Still nothing. Now sensing something might be terribly wrong, he pulled everything out of the safe onto the floor. Still kneeling, Drew picked up the envelopes one by one, reading the labels of each and then tossing each into the hall. Rick's package was gone!

Only one other person knew the combination to the safe—Doug. Hoping against hope that Doug had taken the package by mistake, Drew got up off the floor, picked his way over the mess he just made in the hall, and stormed down to Doug's office.

"Doug, have you been in the safe?" Drew blurted as he burst through Doug's partially closed door.

Startled, Doug took a minute to respond. "What? No!" he said defensively. "What the hell is wrong man, you look like you lost one of your kids at Disney World."

"I put a package, an envelope, full of a client's confidential documents in there a few weeks ago, and now it's not there. Are you sure?" Drew's challenging tone disappeared, now he was pleading.

"I haven't been in there, really. I don't know what you're talking about. Whose documents? What client?" Doug asked.

"A guy I met on the flight back from LA came to see me and wanted my help. He said he was looking at opening a business and selling some advanced aircraft stuff. He gave me this packet of documents to keep safe until he could move to Huntsville or someplace and get up and running. Then yesterday this FBI agent comes here wanting to find this guy. Since I represent him, I couldn't tell them much. Hell, I don't know where he is, I haven't heard from him."

"What guy? This is a client?" Doug obviously had a million questions. Most of which Drew wouldn't be able to answer.

"Rick Donnelly," Drew said. "The guy's name is Rick Donnelly."

Several blocks to the North, one of Agent Frank Deal's agents pulled a set of headphones off one ear. Over her right shoulder the agent said, "He knows."

THIRTY-ONE

After the successful infiltration and search of Drew Campbell's law office, it took only minutes for Deal's team to return to base. Deal immediately took the documents out of the envelope found in Drew Campbell's safe. Maintaining strict evidence handling protocol, the team scanned each document into the computer before beginning the lengthy process of scanning for fingerprints and other evidence left behind by whoever handled the documents.

After Deal's tech team finished with each page, Deal laid the documents one by one on a long table for further examination. Most of the documents were clearly copies of blueprints or technical wiring diagrams for various parts of an aircraft. He had been broadly familiarized with the GW-FB1 fighter-bomber and its propulsion system. The airframe of the GW-FB1 was unremarkable, even standard construction. Deal realized he was looking at the plans for the airframe itself—cockpit, landing gear, and weapons systems. But, despite reviewing every document twice, Deal and his team found nothing depicting or even describing the gravity wave generator or the reactor that powered it. And, the one item they needed to locate most, the process for manufacturing Element 128, just wasn't there.

Of course, this didn't necessarily lead to the conclusion the 128 processing information was never in the packet of documents. Deal's team spent hours reviewing the results of their forensic examination. Rick Donnelly's fingerprints were present on both the envelope and almost every document. Drew Campbell's fingerprints were lifted from the envelope, but none of the other documents. Campbell could certainly have removed documents after he received it from Donnelly, but Deal didn't think this so. Deal suspected the team would find Donnelly's DNA on the glue holding the envelope shut. Plus, Deal knew in his gut that Campbell had no idea what Donnelly had given him.

Standing in front of the table covered with documents, Deal contemplated the fact that the break-in, while successfully executed, did not obtain the stolen Element 128 processing data. The only two people that could re-create the process, Donnelly and Knox, were still missing. Plus, the only lead they had was Donnelly's connection to Campbell. He had no choice but to continue concentrating his efforts in that direction. But now, he had to report.

Deal walked to the other side of the headquarters space to gain a semblance of privacy. Opening his phone he said, "Director." The phone's voice recognition system uploaded a very private number and after just two rings Director William B. Glover picked up.

"Glover," the director answered.

"Director, Agent Deal. We have recovered documents that were in the possession of Donnelly's attorney, Drew Campbell. Unfortunately, the missing processing information was not included in those documents."

"I don't suppose I want to know how you 'recovered' these documents, do I Agent Deal?" the director asked.

"Probably not, sir. We will continue our relationship with Mr. Campbell in case Donnelly attempts to make contact. Knox has gone to ground and has not reappeared," Deal reported.

"Very well. We've been unable to establish any electronic link to either Donnelly or Knox. Even the NSA is pulling its hair out on this one. OK, keep me informed, I'll brief the president." The director ended the call.

Under most circumstances, even combat, Agent Frank Deal was not prone to displays of emotion. But, standing in the darkened headquarters early that morning, Deal allowed himself one "Shit!" but under his breath. Turning back to his team, he said, "OK people, what are we missing? Is it Campbell? Is he working with Donnelly, or is he just a dupe? Let's get back on this. I want Campbell's files and computers combed in detail. Anything, and I mean anything that could be related to Donnelly in any way I want to see immediately. It's been a long night, and it's going to be a long day, but we don't have the luxury of time. Get to it."

THIRTY-TWO

Dave Knox's cell phone sprang suddenly to life, vibrating and ringing with the incessant clamor of a phone in a 1950s French brothel. Startled, he almost dropped his tray of test tubes. Dave chastised himself for the millionth time for not choosing a less intrusive ringtone.

"Whoa! That was close!" Dave said to nobody. Putting the tray down carefully on a long table, Dave dug in the pocket of his lab coat for the irritating device. Finally freeing it from his pocket, he quickly swiped across its face to stop the blaring.

"Where the goddamn hell is he?" Dave recognized the pissed-off voice of Governor Franks immediately. After talking with Rick earlier that day, he forgot to call Franks with an update.

"Margie, is that you?" Dave asked, smiling, and knowing it would elicit a reaction.

"You're goddamn right it's me you eggheaded prick. Where's Donnelly?"

"Margie, Margie, calling me names is so unwarranted. Now calm down. Rick called me earlier and he'll be here by tomorrow afternoon. He sounded like himself again. There's nothing to worry about. I know him better than anyone and there's no way he would miss this great opportunity. Trust me, it's all cool. Anyway, you know eggheads, we can be difficult."

Governor Franks was not appeased. She wanted details, when Donnelly called, where he was, what he was doing, and how he was getting to Austin. Dave explained that Rick was near Memphis by now and would be driving down the next day. Rick just wanted to hang out there for the night.

"Margie, he called earlier but I got busy. When I'm deep into some cool chemistry, I lose track of about everything else. So, take the afternoon off and go shoot some defenseless animal with one of your great big guns," Dave chided her.

"Screw, you," the governor responded. "If you talk to him again, you tell him The Doyens insist on coming to get him, wherever he is. If he's not here goddamn soon, *you* might just be the defenseless turd I shoot with my great big gun!"

Franks hung up. Dave just smiled to himself and went back to work. He really couldn't help messing with Margie. The Klass's plans and ambitions wouldn't be worth a damn without him. Anyway, Dave knew Margie liked him, mostly because he wasn't afraid of her, unlike everyone else.

Franks thought Dave was, in fact, an eggheaded prick. But, she had to give him credit. It took some gold-plated cast iron cajones to steal plans for the GW-FB1 from under the government's nose. On top of that, he was instrumental in developing the Element 128 manufacturing process. He had a right to be cocky, but he sure grated on her nerves.

Despite Dave's assurances, Franks wasn't satisfied. She didn't like details left unattended. And she couldn't let Rick run around the countryside freely based on Knox's judgment about how he sounded on the phone. Franks decided she needed to manage this her own way—personally.

Franks placed a call to the Texas Ranger Division. Disbanded by the federal government during the Reconstruction Era after the Civil War, the Texas Rangers now have police jurisdiction over the entire state of Texas. Once the Texas Rangers rode after outlaws and bandits on horseback. Today, the Rangers use state-of-the-art law enforcement technology to investigate criminal activity. Along with its broad-based authority, the Rangers are also charged with the personal protection of the governor of Texas. Franks recently promoted the chief of the Rangers to his current position. Also a long-time friend, Chief Sam Snow owed Franks more than he could hope to repay. Snow would have obeyed orders from the governor anyway, but Franks was also one of The Doyens, and Snow was a patriot.

After a short explanation about the urgent need to locate Donnelly, Franks asked what Snow needed to track him down. Snow's response was simple—Donnelly's cell phone number. While the FBI's search for Donnelly stalled without the ability to track his burner cell phone, Dave Knox's phone had recorded the number just hours ago. If Rick still had the phone, Snow could locate him within twenty feet. Franks ordered Snow to make it happen.

Snow's tech team retrieved the number from Knox's phone, irking him greatly for interrupting his work. Snow explained that they were just going to make sure Rick was safe. Dave was too busy to worry about it. The Texas Rangers' tech team then easily triangulated the position of Rick's phone from several cellular tower signals. Snow reported back to Franks in less than ninety minutes.

"Governor, Mr. Donnelly's cell phone is currently on and operating," Snow said over an encrypted line to the governor's office.

"He told Knox he was in Tennessee somewhere. So where is that SOB?" Franks asked.

"No, Madam Governor, he is not. If Donnelly's holding the phone with that number, he's just outside Tuscaloosa, Alabama. We put him at a Hillmont Inn on the north side of I-twenty/fifty-nine off exit number seventy-seven. We will continue to monitor his location until you order otherwise," Snow replied, masking his pride.

"Goddamn! Good job Snow. Keep me informed." Franks hung up the phone.

Franks sat back in her over-sized leather office chair and put both hands behind her beautifully styled short gray hair. The office reserved for the governor of Texas rivals the Oval Office itself. The magnificent room is adorned with rich blue rugs and oversized green leather furnishings. An immense painting depicting the heroic defense of the Alamo by freedom-seeking Texans rises over ten feet and covers one entire wall. Franks' ornate and massive eight-by-four-foot desk dominated the other side of the room. The office and its decor made all who entered feel small, just as intended. Looking at the painting of the Alamo again she thought, *Those Texans knew what freedom really meant and were willing to pay for it. Well so am I.*

Franks took another moment to consider her options. She weighed Dave Knox's opinion that Donnelly was a true believer and patriot against the plain fact that Donnelly lied. Never reticent to make a decision, Franks picked up the phone and told one of her three assistants to get Governor Smith of Alabama on the phone immediately—and that she didn't give a damn how it was done. She replaced the receiver and waited.

A few minutes later her phone rang. Picking up the receiver again, her chief of staff informed her that Governor Smith was on the private line.

"Governor Smith, thank you for taking the time to speak with me," Franks said.

"Governor Franks, I am at your service. Is there something I can do to assist you this afternoon?"

Franks, as always, got right to the point. "Governor, who do we have in Tuscaloosa that can fix a problem?"

THIRTY-THREE

Hunter Dodson III's cell phone rang at eight-thirty PM that same evening. Dodson looked at the number calling, immediately pushed back his chair, excused himself, and walked out onto the streets of New York City. Dodson flew to New York that morning with his parents to attend a new Broadway production and spend a few days shopping. The trip was his mother's idea, and she insisted Hunter and his older sister accompany them. Hunter didn't mind going to New York, but he detested shopping. He and his father would be going to a Yankee's game instead.

Walking outside, Dodson answered, "Yes, sir. Good afternoon."

The distinctly curt voice of Governor G. Hunt Smith said, "Mr. Dodson, are you in the middle of a traffic jam or somethin'? I can hardly hear you!"

"No sir," Dodson replied. "I'm in New York with my parents. What can I do for you sir?" Hunter placed a hand over one ear and stepped back into the relative quiet of restaurant's entrance.

"Oh, I see, well first, be sure to give your father and lovely mother my regards," Smith said, always the politician. Hunter Dodson Jr. donated heavily to Klass candidates. The governor continued. "We have a serious and rather immediate problem in Tuscaloosa. Since you aren't there, do you have someone we can trust to undertake a, uh, delicate assignment? One that might require some amount of, um, persuasion?"

Hunter listened closely. *The governor of Alabama, one of The Doyens, was asking for his help directly and he wasn't in the state! Goddammit! He needed to get whatever Smith needed done! As the current Chairman of The Tyros control committee at Alabama, it was his job to handle orders from The Doyens, but at the moment, he was out of position!* He decided to use this as an opportunity to show the reach of his influence.

"Yes, sir," Hunter replied immediately. "I'll get whatever it is handled. I've got a good team."

"Someone will call you in precisely ten minutes with details. Be available," Smith ordered.

Hunter went back to his table and asked if his parents would mind if he went back to the room to handle some business in Tuscaloosa. While his mother began to protest, his father put his hand on his wife's shoulder and said understandingly, "Sure son, we'll catch up with you shortly."

Hunter quickly returned to his hotel on Central Park South, just a block away. He found a quiet seat in the lobby and waited for what he knew would be a secure call. Just a minute after sitting down his phone rang again. His phone identified the caller as "William Simmons." The caller didn't identify himself, or even waste time with the social convention of saying hello. He simply began describing what needed to be done and when. Hunter listened, absorbing the details. When he was finished the caller asked, "Questions?"

Hunter said, "No. I'll report to the usual number afterward." Hunter ended the call and immediately found Jimbo's number in his contacts.

"What the hell?" Jimbo said when his phone rang. Jimbo was settled on his couch, with a big blonde girl straddling his lap. They were both fully clothed, a condition Jimbo planned to remedy shortly. Jimbo said, "Hold on a sec there honey," and reached across the couch for his phone. Looking at the number, Jimbo pushed the girl to the side and stood up.

"This better be good. I'm sorta busy here," Jimbo said by way of answering the call.

"Tough nuts Jimbo. Lose whatever drunk chick is there and pull up your pants. The Doyens need our help. And, we'll need The Boys," Hunter said.

THIRTY-FOUR

"What the hell are you talkin' about Hunter?" Jimbo asked. "And why do you sound nervous?"

"I'm not screwing around Jimbo," Hunter said. "I got a call a few minutes ago. The Doyens have ordered us to pick up a guy named Donnelly, Rick Donnelly, and it's real important this gets done and that it gets done tonight. I'm in New York, so it's up to you. We got no choice here. I don't like it, but we have to get this guy and hold on to him for a day or so. He ain't gonna want to go, so you'll need some muscle."

Jimbo turned his back and walked across the room so his date couldn't overhear him. "Dang Dodson, tonight? Don't they have some pro or something that takes care of this kind of thing? I mean, I don't know anything about grabbing someone and keeping him locked down. Really? This ain't funny. This is real go-to-prison kind of stuff," he complained softly.

"Look Jimbo, quit being a whiney bitch, we get this done and we're made. You want to be governor one day? I'm tellin' you, they need this bad. Call The Boys and get J.P. on it. All you have to do is manage the thing, just like you did with the O'Dell bitch. Y'all did good with that so you're the man for the job. If you can't handle it, I'll find someone else with more guts," threatened Hunter.

"OK. OK. Give me the details," Jimbo agreed, still shaken by the lunatic orders but unwilling to be labeled as a coward.

Hunter took the next couple of minutes explaining that Rick Donnelly was staying at the Hillmont near the interstate. The Doyens needed him secured until sometime tomorrow afternoon, when he could be transferred to a team from Texas for transportation out of state. Jimbo wrote down a few notes and ended the call.

"Babe, bring me that bottle. I need a drink. Sorry, but I got business, we'll have to do this another time," She pouted, but brought him the bottle of Jack Daniels and his half-full glass.

The girl left and Jimbo sat brooding for ten minutes while he polished off a couple of drinks to build his courage. Feeling better than he probably should, Jimbo called J.P. and explained the basics. They agreed to meet at the 8-Ball Truck Stop in thirty minutes. The 8-Ball had the best twenty-four-hour breakfast in town and students often ended a night of beer drinking there to soak up excess alcohol. After one more drink, Jimbo realized he had a problem. He couldn't drive across town on his own. If he got pulled over, this job would be screwed and more important, he would never recover with The Doyens. He needed a driver, someone that owned him a favor, and would keep quiet.

Jimbo grabbed his phone and keys, walked down one floor and knocked on Zach Self's door. Zach was studying for a history exam and luckily for Jimbo, hadn't been drinking.

"Self," Jimbo said, "I need a ride out to the 8-Ball."

"I'd like to Jimbo, but I got a lot to do tonight, I got an early exam and I still have to…"

"Look man, this is important," Jimbo interrupted impatiently. "This is one of those times when The Tyros needs you, just like we talked about. So, if you have any hope of moving up, you need to just shut up and move! Now, get your stuff and let's go."

Zach didn't understand what was wrong with Jimbo. Sure, he'd obviously been drinking, but he wasn't plastered. Plus, Jimbo never worried about drinking and driving. But, for whatever reason, he wanted a ride tonight and he owed Jimbo a favor—probably a lot of favors. So he decided that if Jimbo needed a ride, he would do it.

"OK, Jimbo. No problem. Let me get my wallet and we'll take off," Zach said. Zach grabbed his things and followed Jimbo down the stairs and out to Zach's Nissan Sentra.

"Oh no," Jimbo commented. "I'm not ridin' in your little rice cooker. Here, we'll take my truck." Jimbo tossed his keys to Zach. "Try drivin' a real man's vehicle for a change."

Zach climbed up into the cab while Jimbo swung his oversize frame into the passenger seat. Not used to driving anything this big, Zach carefully backed up and then pulled out onto University Boulevard. They hadn't gone two blocks before Jimbo told him to pick up the pace. Zach could tell Jimbo's nerves were on edge and carefully asked if everything was OK. Jimbo just nodded and told Zach to hurry up. It was now past nine o'clock in the evening. Traffic was light, so Zach sped up. As soon as he did, Jimbo growled at him to watch the speed limit.

Ten minutes later they pulled into the large parking lot of the 8-Ball. Eighteen-wheel tractor-trailer rigs stood side by side along at one end of the huge lot. The immense, round neon-lighted 8-Ball sign shined above their heads like a full moon that was way too close to the earth. Dozens of halogen lights mounted on tall poles and the florescent fixtures over the pumps provided blotchy light over the rest of the lot.

"Pull around back," Jimbo ordered. "Over there," he said pointing to the farthest corner from the tractor-trailer rigs.

Zach drove slowly past the big rigs in the direction Jimbo pointed. A couple of vehicles were already there, a pickup and what looked like a new muscle car of some kind sporting bright lime green paint and black racing stripes running over the hood, roof, and trunk deck. Jimbo told him to stop about twenty feet from the other vehicles.

"Stay in the truck. This is going to take a few minutes, so chill out here," Jimbo said with no humor at all.

"Yeah, OK, what's going on?" Zach asked. "Who are those guys?"

"Just some guys I know. I have to discuss a little business with them that ain't none of your business. Just do what I said. I'll be back," Jimbo said as he opened the door. Zach had no idea what was going on, but he hoped like hell this wasn't Jimbo's dope dealer or something. Jimbo could be a loose cannon, most often after he'd been downing Jack Daniels. Zach rolled his window down. Maybe he could hear what was going on. If this was a drug buy, he wanted to know it. He said he would stay in the truck, he didn't promise not to try and find out what this was all about.

Jimbo waved, friendly like, as he walked toward the two other vehicles. The door of the green car opened and J.P. Hoffman, the First Man of The Boys, stepped out. J.P. wore jeans and an old black T-shirt, but his clothes couldn't hide his ripped physique. J.P.'s blonde hair was cut so short he appeared nearly bald. Part of a tattoo peaked from under the neckline of his shirt and his lower arms sported a colorful mix of fire, dragons, and skulls.

Nobody else appeared from J.P.'s car or the truck. Both Jimbo and J.P. acted completely nonchalant. J.P. stuck out his hand as Jimbo approached and gave a fake smile. The two shook hands and then rested their backs against the side of J.P.'s car. J.P. lit a cigarette.

"Nice ride, J.P. New?" Jimbo asked.

"Yep, had it less than a week. My grandmother, bless her heart, thought I needed a new car. This here's a Hellcat, 707 horses. Good ol' Grandma!" J.P. explained patting the roof of his new car. "OK, let's cut the bullshit, what's the deal? We gotta nab some guy or somethin'?"

Jimbo crossed his arms and explained their orders came straight from The Doyens through Hunter Dodson. They needed a scientist named Rick Donnelly picked up and held until tomorrow afternoon. Donnelly was supposed to be at the Hillmont Inn one exit up from where they stood. Jimbo described him as a normal white guy, brown hair, usually wears glasses. They had no description for his car. Most importantly, Donnelly could not be hurt in any way. Once picked up, they were to protect him at all costs.

Not seeming a bit concerned, J.P. asked, "And they think Donnelly is at the Hillmont? Got any idea what they want him so bad for?"

"I got no idea. All I know is what I told you. He was at the hotel a few hours ago. I'm supposed to call this number for an update. Wherever he is now, we have to find him and wrap him up for a few hours. You got some help?" Jimbo inquired. He was supposed to be in charge of this little rodeo, so he figured he better ask.

"Oh yeah. Plenty," J.P. said motioning vaguely at the truck next to his car. " And *we* aren't doing anything, I am. You've done your job. Make your call. Let's see if he's still where he's suppose to be."

Jimbo dialed the number Hunter had given him. The person answering simply said, "Yes."

Jimbo said, "I'm supposed to call for an update on the location of Rick… our subject." *Crap, he almost blew it right there! He wasn't supposed to use names.*

A few seconds later the voice at the other end said, "Same location confirmed."

Jimbo ended the call and confirmed Donnelly's location for J.P.

"We'll take it from here. I'll give you a call when we've bagged this hombre," J.P. said as he turned and reached for the door handle of the Challenger.

"Hold on J.P.," Jimbo said, grabbing the sleeve of J.P.'s T-shirt. "It's my ass on the line here, maybe I better follow you over there."

J.P. slapped Jimbo's hand off his shirt, spun to his right, locked Jimbo's right hand behind his back, and pushed Jimbo's face hard into the roof of the car.

"Listen up Jimbo. Touch me again and I'll find a nice quiet piece of woods to hide your fat dead ass in. Got it?" J.P. hissed into Jimbo's ear as he shoved even harder on the side of Jimbo's head. "I said I'll take care of it from here. I don't need you hanging around to bitch about how it gets done. Ya hear?"

Through clenched teeth Jimbo croaked, "Yeah. Yeah. OK."

J.P. let Jimbo up. Jimbo, still dazed at how fast J.P. moved, said, "Fine. But they need Donnelly alive and in good health. It's your ass if it don't go right."

"No, it's *our* ass," J.P. said turning away again and getting into his car.

Jimbo stepped back as J.P. started the engine. An unholy wail spat from the tail pipes, followed by a high-pitched whine. The rear tires spun in place, shooting a cloud of smoke into the night air. Before Jimbo could take another step back, J.P.'s car shot forward toward the exit, followed by the pickup.

So much for sneakin' around, Jimbo thought as he turned back to his own truck.

Zach watched the entire scene unfold. He didn't catch much of the conversation, but he did hear J.P. say something about grabbing a guy named Donald or Donny, or something like that. It looked like a friendly meeting, right up until Jimbo got body slammed against the car. Zach very briefly considered trying to help, but before he could decide what to do, Jimbo got up and the other guy was in his car and leaving. He quickly rolled the window up and started the truck. Zach would readily admit he took advantage of every circumstance that even leaned toward benefiting him in some fashion. But despite his ambition and opportunism, Zach didn't like what he had just seen and heard. This felt bad. Real bad.

Jimbo climbed back into the cab rubbing the side of his face.

"You OK, man?" Zach asked, covering his own anxiety with feigned ignorance. "Who was that? He moved like a ninja."

"Shut up," Jimbo said. "None of this happened, you understand? You didn't drive me nowhere tonight, and you didn't see nothin'. This is private stuff, and if I hear you opened your mouth about it...just don't make me have to decide what to do to you."

"OK. OK. I get it. Back to the house?" Zach asked, now ready for this night just to be over.

"Yeah," Jimbo said. "I need a drink."

THIRTY-FIVE

J.P. and one of The Boys, who went by Skeeter, rode in J.P.'s Challenger Hellcat. The little brunette, Gina, who had knocked on Mary O'Dell's door pretending to be her neighbor, rode with Dog and Mikey in Mikey's pickup. Just before leaving for the meet with Jimbo, Dog and Mikey had installed a windowless shell on the bed of Mikey's GMC Sierra for covert transportation of their objective. Before leaving The Boys' unofficial headquarters in an abandoned garage near Clanton, Alabama, J.P. made it clear that they were on serious business and that there would be no drinking or pot until the job was finished. None of The Boys would disobey J.P., because doing so would put the offender in the hospital. And that's if J.P. decided to go easy.

They didn't drive directly to the hotel. After burning good rubber out of the 8-Ball, J.P., with Mikey's truck following, drove down the road, and pulled into the parking lot of a fast food place. Mikey pulled up alongside J.P.

J.P. stuck his head out the window and motioned for Dog to open his passenger side window. J.P. told him, "Get down to the Hillmont and find a spot where you can see all the exits. There's a quiet road right behind there that might be good, but if you can't see both exits, send Mikey out to watch the other one. If a white guy comes out by himself, call me."

"We got it J.P. We'll be watching," Dog replied.

"It's late, so if he's there, he's probably there to stay. Don't screw this up," J.P. said pointing at Dog and then Mikey. "Get goin'."

After Mikey's truck left, J.P. sat back against the seat and lit another cigarette. Leaning his head back against the headrest, he said without looking at his companion, "Skeeter, how do we do this?"

Skeeter, who got his moniker from the initials of his real name, Frederick Leonard Yeager, possessed the mind of a genius, but the personality of a mad scientist. Skeeter resembled the tiny insect he was named after. Skinny to the point of emaciation, his clothes hung limply off every part of his body. He wore round wire-rimmed eyeglasses that made his eyes look half again larger than normal and his hair was an uncontrollable brown greasy mess.

Despite his odd appearance, Skeeter was invaluable. The Boys had expertise in weaponry and combat, but not much in the way of brainpower. Skeeter used his knowledge of chemistry, engineering, and computer science to keep a string of automated meth-cookers operating around the clock. Also a genius strategist, Skeeter had mastered chess before he turned seven years old. His mind automatically ordered future events by probability of occurrence, and then chose the course of action most likely to result in success. J.P. turned to Skeeter whenever he needed a plan.

Skeeter sat looking out the side window away from J.P., his fingers combing through his hair over and over. J.P. knew this meant Skeeter's mind was hard at work. Rushing him would only cause him to lash out in a verbal torrent of expletives. Nope, J.P. would wait. It didn't take long.

Skeeter finally spoke up. "We know that Mr. Donnelly's phone was positioned within the hotel, presumably in a guest room. Even assuming he checked in using his real name, which is so unlikely that the proposition should be immediately dismissed, hotel security will not divulge his room number. Since we do not know what name he used, force applied to the hotel staff will yield no acceptable result. If he is within the hotel, and we cannot locate his room, then we must have him come out of the building on his own accord. Thus we have two options, bring him out on a ruse through a call to his cell phone, which will fail since he is most likely not expecting a call; or, cause a condition that will surely have all occupants of the hotel leave the building. Once they are outside, we can eliminate couples, families, hotel staff, blacks, and other minorities. The odds favor an acceptably small number of white single males appearing outside that can then be approached for identification of Mr. Donnelly."

While J.P. didn't mind listening to Skeeter's long verbal explanations of his logic, he just needed to know how Skeeter proposed to make this thing happen. "So, how do we get everyone out of the place?" he asked.

Skeeter looked at J.P. with a puzzled look on his face. "Why, set it on fire of course."

THIRTY-SIX

Zach could tell Jimbo was shaken up and angry at the same time. All the way back to the house, Jimbo just looked out the side window of the truck, absentmindedly rubbing his face where it had come into contact with the roof of J.P.'s car. Zach tried to make sense of what he had seen and heard. He didn't understand how or why Jimbo was associated with those guys. God, he thought, *the one that hammered on Jimbo looked like one of those neo-Nazis or KKK idiots he had seen on T.V.* But, what bothered him most was the snippet of conversation about grabbing some guy. He couldn't quite make out the name when it happened, but he knew it was something like "Donny." *And, what did they mean by "grabbing"?* Zach thought for a moment they might have meant picking him up or something, *but if that was the case, why the clandestine meeting place?* No, he concluded, *that little meeting wasn't about anything innocent. Oh God, please don't let me be mixed up with something really bad*, he prayed silently. But he knew it was already too late.

Zach kept himself together on the way back into town and as he parked the truck at the house. "OK, I'm headed back to the books. I still got a history test tomorrow," Zach said as off- handedly as he could. He started to open the door when Jimbo grabbed his arm. Zach turned around about to yank his arm away. Then he saw Jimbo's eyes. Zach had never seen Jimbo like this; he looked nearly crazed and a bruise was already appearing on the side of his face.

"I meant what I said before. None of this is your business," Jimbo snarled.

Zach had had enough. He yanked his arm out of Jimbo's grip. "Fine. I heard you the first time. Here's your keys, I gotta study." Zach responded with more ferocity than he thought he could muster. He tossed the keys on the seat, opened the door, and stepped down from the truck. Without looking back, he walked through the front door of the house, went straight to his room, and locked the door. His roommate, as usual, wasn't there. Probably spending the night at his girlfriend's apartment again.

Zach sat down on his bed and put his head in his hands. He had to decide what to do. Or, what not to do. The politician in him wanted him to keep his mouth shut, just like Jimbo told him. If he crossed Jimbo, he could also cross off his plans for becoming president of SGA one day and probably a lot of other things as well. This felt different though. This was real life, not college crap. Zach couldn't shake the feeling something horrible and probably criminal was going to happen tonight. Finally setting his political worries aside, he decided he needed to do something, even though it probably meant his plans for the future would be totally flushed down the toilet.

Zach picked up his phone and sent a text to Michael. Ever since they were kids, it was always Michael who had the level head. *Hell*, he thought,

Michael should be called "ice man." Plus, he trusted Michael, more than anyone else in the world, his own father especially included.

'Hey, you around?' his text read.

Michael responded, 'Yep. In my room working on a paper.'

'Can I come up?'

'Sure,' Michael responded. 'J out for the night. The usual.' Michael's oversexed roommate would not be there.

Zach made sure he had his keys, wallet, and phone. Then he cracked the heavy door just enough to look down the hall. He didn't want to risk running into Jimbo. Finding the hall deserted, he moved quickly to the stairwell. After looking up and hearing nothing, he bounded up the stairs two at a time to the next floor. He waited for a moment before entering the hall when he heard voices. Zach didn't want to chance having to answer any questions if one of the brothers happened to see him leave or return with Jimbo earlier. When he was sure the hall was clear, he walked down to Michael's room and knocked. Michael pulled the door open from inside without getting out of his desk chair. Zach stepped in quickly, shut the door, and locked it. Zach's heart beat against his chest like a drum and he had a hard time catching his breath.

Michael swiveled around in his chair, about to make some smart comment about Zach being needy, when he saw the fear and conflict in Zach's eyes. Michael knew his best friend's personality top to bottom and something definitely wasn't right.

"Maybe you better sit down," Michael suggested. "You look like someone's out to murder you."

Zach hadn't been looking at Michael. He just stood staring at the door. After a second, he looked around and realized Michael had said something. All he could muster right then was, "Huh?"

"You look like you've seen a goddamn ghost. Sit your ass down. What's going on?"

Zach finally reacted to Michael's prompting and plopped down onto the edge of the bottom bunk. He ran his hand through his straight black hair, a sure sign he was upset. A stray strand fell back onto his forehead. Michael just watched, letting Zach catch up with himself.

"Hey buddy, what's going on?" Michael asked again.

Now it came rushing out of Zach all at once. "I dunno. I mean, yeah, something bad. I think anyway. I don't know. A little while ago Jimbo came to my room and asked me to drive him out to the 8-Ball. He'd been drinking, not wasted, but you know Jimbo. Anyway, I told him I had to study, but well, he knew I owed him, so I said, yeah, sure. He wanted to take his truck for some reason, so I drove him out there. I didn't know why he needed to go, he just said he had to meet some guys on business and I shouldn't worry about it. So I did, anyway, then it got weird...we..."

"OK. OK. Slow down. So Jimbo got you to drive him out to the truck stop. No big deal. What happened then?" Michael asked, trying to calm Zach enough to get the story out in some understandable fashion.

Zach, now somewhat recovered, described how they drove around back and parked. Jimbo got out and started talking to a guy that looked like a skinhead or member of the Klan. They only talked for a few minutes.

"And you don't know what it was about? Sounds more stupid than anything really bad so far. What happened next?" Michael asked.

"Well, I wanted to know what was going on, so I rolled my window down to try and hear. I didn't get much, but I did hear Jimbo tell this tattooed Nazi-looking dude that they had to grab and hold onto a guy named Donny, or Donald, or something like that. I'm not being paranoid. If you'd seen this go down, you'd know it was serious business," Zach tried to explain.

"So Jimbo told this skinhead tattooed Nazi to go and grab and hold onto a guy named Donny? Yeah, that's strange, but—" Zach cut him off.

"No man, look, Jimbo got beat up by this guy like it was nothing. Jimbo! Plus, when he got back in the truck he literally threatened me about keeping my mouth shut about the whole thing. I've never seen him like that, ever. I could tell he was scared shitless the whole way back. Before I got out of the truck he grabbed me and threatened me again! This is no joke. If I thought it was no big deal, do you really think I'd be spilling my guts when Jimbo told me not too?" Zach looked like he was getting upset again.

"No, no. OK then, what do you think this is all about?" Michael asked reassuringly.

"I'm pretty sure Jimbo just passed on orders to some kind of criminals to go kidnap a guy."

THIRTY-SEVEN

Michael looked at Zach for a long moment then got up and started pacing back and forth across the small room. Michael thought better on his feet.

Zach's story sounded genuine. No doubt his little trip with Jimbo shook him up. Plus, Zach could read people better than anyone else Michael ever met. If he believed this meeting really scared Jimbo, Michael believed him. Jimbo and his family had many connections and wielded a lot of clout. Michael considered the possibility that they were into some illegal stuff. Maybe drugs or something. One thing was for sure though: Jimbo himself wasn't the mastermind of this or anything else. While he loved to throw his authority around, in the final analysis, Jimbo was just a bully. No, whatever that meeting was really about, it wasn't Jimbo's idea.

"So, what should I do?" Zach asked Michael.

"If you really think something criminal is going to happen, I guess you should call the police," Michael said.

"And tell them what? I drove my drunk frat brother out to the truck stop to meet a bunch of rednecks? And, oh, by the way, I think I heard them say something about kidnapping some guy named Donny?" Zach responded dismissively.

"Yeah, I see your point. It doesn't sound like much when you put it like that. If they didn't believe you,

you'd have accomplished nothing except pissing off Jimbo, and in a real major way," Michael said.

"So, what do we do?" Zach asked again, not challenging Michael, but throwing the question up for grabs.

Michael continued pacing for another minute. Then he stopped.

"Any idea where these guys were going?" he asked Zach.

"I don't know, let me think. We were parked in the back. Jimbo and the other guy were leaning against this bright green car. It had black stripes over the hood and it looked brand-new. It was one of those new old-looking muscle cars. Let's see, they were talking and yeah, I remember Jimbo pointing up the interstate toward Birmingham. Like he was giving directions. Then, huh, he looked like he was describing getting off and going back under the highway. You know, like this." Zach brought his had up then down again and curving back to the left. "Then the other guy looked just across the interstate from where we were, like maybe he could see it from there. I didn't hear anything, but I'm pretty sure they were talking about someplace nearby, just on this side of the highway."

"OK," Michael said slowly. "Sounds like they were going to stay close. What about the car, you don't know what kind it was for sure?"

"No. You're the car nut. But I'd know it again in half a sec if I saw it. Not many cars are painted florescent green. Really nice ride for a really bad-looking dude."

"I think I know the kind of car. Hold on," Michael said moving to his desk and looking under piles of paper and textbooks. Finding a magazine, Michael flipped through the pages. Holding up the magazine he asked Zach, "Is this the car?"

"Yeah, that's it! Definitely," Zach answered right away.

"Dodge Challenger. Yeah, no wonder you would recognize it again. Badass ride for sure." Michael said. Then, looking up at Zach with a little smile he said, "Let's go."

"Go? Go where?" Zach said.

"Let's go see if we can find it."

THIRTY-EIGHT

Rick Donnelly's long drive to Tuscaloosa gave him time to ponder his situation. He didn't doubt for a moment the FBI, counter-intelligence agencies, and probably every police officer in the country were all hunting for him. But his trip from Columbia, South Carolina, had been completely uneventful, even boring. His old truck ran down the interstates at 70 miles per hour, and he would be in Tuscaloosa in less than an hour. He felt surprisingly good. Yet, he didn't let down his guard.

Rick's outstanding ability to conquer any scientific problem worked to his advantage. He wanted to prop up his back story about starting a business so Drew Campbell wouldn't get suspicious and he'd keep his little packet of insurance safe. Afterward, he would drive directly to Austin and continue work on the Element 128 project with Dave Knox. He looked forward to getting back into a lab, the one place where he always felt at home.

Rick wasn't going to take any chances while in Tuscaloosa though. If the FBI had connected him to Drew, he might be walking into an ambush. Rick had been careful to use only cash now for weeks. He was off the grid, so to speak, except for his limited-use cell phone. Rick planned to dump the phone and approach Drew when he was alone.

Seeing a Hillmont Inn advertised at the next exit, Rick pulled off the interstate and drove into the hotel's parking lot. He found a space facing a blank wall and killed the engine. He got out of the truck, stretched, and pretended to look in the bed for something, all the while scanning for anyone nearby and for the presence of security cameras. Satisfied he wasn't being observed, Rick pulled a small duffle bag up out of the bed, carried it around to the front of the truck, and looked through it. A very narrow strip of grass and thick short bushes separated the parking lot from the building. Rick pulled the cell phone out of the duffle and simply placed it behind a bush. After closing the bag, he stood and looked around as if confused, tossed the bag back in the bed of the truck and drove away. Anyone actually tracking the phone would place him at the hotel.

When daylight savings time ends in central Alabama, darkness falls by five in the afternoon. It was four-forty-five when Rick decided to try and catch Drew before he left the office. Actually going to the office would be a bad idea, given his concern that it was at least possible he had been associated with Drew. Rick already had a map of Tuscaloosa and Drew's address memorized. It was a simple matter to drive near his building, park in an unobtrusive spot, and follow Drew when he left. Rick was betting on Drew being a creature of habit.

After a short drive across town, Rick parked a block away from Drew's office building. From his location, Rick could clearly see the sign stating HAMNER

& CAMPBELL, P.C. through his windshield. Rick remembered Drew drove a black BMW 5 Series sedan and one of the three cars still at the office matched that description. Rick didn't have to wait long.

Rick sat quietly in his truck until he saw Drew walk out the front door and around the building carrying what looked to be a gym bag. Drew wore a pair of khaki slacks and a light blue long-sleeve shirt. Despite the chilly temperature, he didn't have a jacket. Now Rick needed his luck to hold one more time. If Drew would just stop on the way home somewhere, anywhere, Rick would have a chance to talk to him directly.

Drew drove right by Rick when he left. All Rick had to do was pull away from the curb, make a quick u-turn, and follow at a discreet distance. As he hoped, Drew drove only five blocks before pulling into the YMCA off Paul Bear Bryant Drive. Rick quickly pulled in a few seconds later and found a parking spot close by. He was out of the truck and walking toward Drew before Drew even opened his door.

"Hey, Drew!" Rick called waiving when Drew got out of his car.

Drew looked around when he heard his name. Then it hit him, *Rick!* A million questions immediately exploded in Drew's head. *What the hell is Rick doing here? Why here? Was Rick following him? Should he be scared?* As Rick walked closer Drew realized he wasn't scared, more perplexed about the reason for Rick's sudden appearance and what he should do about it.

"Hey, Drew!" Rick said again. Drew could see he was smiling. "Hey, sorry about tracking you down like this. I meant to call your office earlier today, but I got all wrapped up with a contractor and then my phone died on me." Rick stuck out his hand.

"Uh, wow, how did you know I was coming here?" Drew asked as he shook Rick's hand.

"A lot of hard detective work," Rick kidded. "Nah, I happened to see you pull out of the office just as I was driving up. I was just hoping to see you for a minute while I was nearby. Sorry if I spooked you."

"No. Just surprised I guess. Since you went to all this trouble, why don't you come inside and we can sit for a minute? I was going to do a short workout before heading home, but I'm not in a rush," Drew suggested. He couldn't avoid the guy, so he had no real choice. Plus, if he had to spend some time with Rick, he wanted it to be in public.

"Sure. Kinda cold anyway. I won't take up your workout time."

They walked into the building and Drew led them to an open area where a few tables and chairs sat beside vending machines.

As they sat down Rick said, "Sorry again about just showing up like this. I know it's weird, but I didn't want to miss the chance to tell you where I am on the business and stuff."

"Rick," Drew said, not buying Rick's cheerful act, "what's really going on?"

Rick could tell Drew wasn't happy with his surprise appearance. "OK," he said, trying to look like he was going to come clean. "I'm in a little trouble. Those documents I gave you are my work, my designs, but they actually belong to Pratt & Whitney. I took them because they weren't being fair with me. What I gave you is just a backup, but now P&W has accused me of corporate espionage. That's not your problem, I understand."

Drew didn't say anything for a few moments. He needed the time to consider his options. On one hand, Rick was his client, and he owed Rick a duty of loyalty, to do what was best for Rick. On the other, the FBI considered the man sitting across the table to be a thief, traitor, and maybe even a murderer. The only thing Drew knew for sure was that he wanted no part of any of it.

Drew now began speaking softly to avoid anyone overhearing the conversation. "You're wrong Rick. It is my problem. You made it my problem by hiring me and giving me those documents. Now listen. This is important. A week or two after we met in Birmingham, the FBI came to see me. I have to tell you that because I'm your lawyer. My advice is to find another lawyer who can effectively represent you and turn yourself in. I can't represent you for that. I don't want to and I'm not qualified even if I did."

Rick's blood instantly froze solid. But thankfully his mind didn't freeze up as well. He had to find out what the FBI knew and then get out of town.

"The FBI!" Rick said, not having to feign surprise. "What did they want? I have no idea why they'd be involved!"

"I think you know what they wanted. They wanted you, and they were all kinds of serious about it," Drew said.

"Did you give them my plans?" Rick asked quickly.

"No. I couldn't tell them anything because of our attorney-client relationship; which, by the way, is now at an end. All I could do, and all I did, was tell them we met on the plane, we ate dinner in Birmingham, and that you hired me as your counsel," Drew said. "So don't tell me anything else, starting right now, that you don't want them to know. Our relationship is over. I'll send your entire retainer back when I get to the office in the morning. Do you understand what I'm telling you?"

"Yeah, I get it. Are you going to tell them I was here? And what about my documents?"

"The answer to the first question is I don't know. As for your documents, I don't have them," Drew said simply.

"What? I thought you said you didn't give them to the feds. Where are they?" Rick said with both fear and the beginnings of panic in his voice.

"I put them in my safe immediately after we met just as you asked. But when I checked the morning after the FBI came to my office, they were gone. Stolen. Only me and my partner have the combination to that safe and he didn't take them. I'm sorry, I just don't know what happened or how they could have gone missing," Drew said honestly.

"I don't know what to say. I don't think I believe you," Rick said, getting up from the table.

"That's the truth, regardless of what you believe," Drew replied, staying in his seat.

Rick had already turned and was walking quickly toward the door.

"Where do you want me to send your money?" Drew called after him.

"Keep it," Rick said over his shoulder as he opened the front door and disappeared into the dark parking lot.

Drew didn't follow him out. There wasn't any reason to and he didn't want to take a chance on what Rick might do. Drew just wanted to get home, have a glass of wine, and talk to Lex about what he should do. Again.

THIRTY-NINE

"Unbelievable. Just unbelievable! He just showed up at the Y?" Lex commented after her husband told her about his surprise encounter with Rick Donnelly. "And he admits to taking those plans or whatever from his employer?"

"Yeah. And now he thinks I gave them to the FBI. God, what a mess! I should never have agreed to represent him. Sometimes I surprise myself with just how gullible I really am," Rick said, obviously stressed.

"Don't beat yourself up. It doesn't help and it's not like you were doing anything wrong. He's gone now and so are those damn documents. That should be an end to it, don't you think?" Lex said trying to relieve her husband's anxiety. While usually quite cool and laid-back, this episode with Rick had thrown Drew badly off balance.

"Yeah, I know," Drew partially agreed, sitting down in his favorite chair and taking another sip of red wine. "But somehow or another I got myself tangled up in this, and I don't think it's as easy as walking away."

"Why not? What's left for you to do?" Lex asked, not challenging Drew's prediction, but trying to elicit his thoughts so she could help.

"I think I better call Agent Deal," Drew said.

Little did the couple know that even as they mentioned his name, Agent Frank Deal was mobilizing his team. After listening in on the Campbells' conversation, Deal ordered his agents into vehicles and moving in all directions. Even though substantial time had passed since Campbell's surprise visit from Rick Donnelly ended, if they could got lucky, maybe they could catch up with him. But, Deal also knew it was probably too late. They had no idea which direction Donnelly chose or a description of his vehicle.

Blue Team split up. Blue One drove north on the interstate toward Birmingham while Blue Two took a second vehicle in a northeasterly direction on back roads. Red One jumped into a black Chevrolet SUV and sped south down the interstate toward Jackson, Mississippi. The other two members of Red Team took a fourth vehicle down secondary highways leading directly south, in the general direction of Mobile.

Campbell hadn't called Deal, choosing instead to head home and talk it over with his lawyer-wife. Deal cursed Campbell's reluctance to cooperate. Then he cursed all lawyers, just for good measure.

Deal desperately wanted to drive to Campbell's house for a nice nose-to-nose interrogation right then. But he couldn't. If the lawyer couple found out he had secretly bugged their house, they could make trouble Deal didn't need. No, he would just have to wait for Campbell to call. This entailed summoning every ounce of patience left in his body, which wasn't much.

Thankfully, his phone rang within minutes. Deal picked up his phone and simply said, "Hello?"

"Agent Deal? Drew Campbell."

"Yes, Mr. Campbell. Have you heard from Mr. Donnelly?" Deal asked as cool as a cucumber.

"As a matter of fact, I just saw him less than an hour ago." Drew said.

"You saw him? You mean you met with him?" Deal asked.

"Yes. That's exactly what I mean," Drew replied. "I fired him as a client and he's unhappy with my services. You should know that I told him about your visit to my office. I felt I had to do that since he was my client. He didn't ask about the topic of the conversation, I only confirmed to him I told you nothing privileged. He became upset and left. He didn't give me any idea where he was going."

"We need to talk. But, for right now, do you know what he was driving? It's important," Deal asked.

"Uh, no. Come to think of it I don't have any idea. I left work, pulled into the YMCA parking lot, got out of my car, and there he was," Drew said. "It was dark, but he said he followed me over from my office. I didn't notice what cars where behind me at the time. It's a very short drive."

"Hold on a second please," Deal said. He put Drew on hold, turned around to his staff and ordered them to review all surveillance recordings from around Drew's office for the past three hours. Maybe they got lucky and caught Donnelly on camera.

Deal took Drew off hold and asked, "Can we meet? I need to see you. It's critical."

"If it's that important, then sure. Where?" Drew responded.

"I can be at your place in fifteen minutes," Deal suggested.

"No, my family is here. How about my office? I can be there in about fifteen minutes anyway," Drew said.

"Fine," Deal agreed. "I'll meet you there."

Deal turned to his operators again. "Anything?"

"Nothing yet, sir. But it doesn't look good. We started with the time frame 4:30 to 5:30 p.m. There was a lot of traffic. We saw Campbell leaving at 5:12 p.m. Our cameras recorded nothing that looked like he was followed after he left. We'll keep checking," the lead technical agent reported.

"Keep trying. See if the YMCA has cameras covering the parking lot and check every route from Campbell's office to the YMCA to see if there are any traffic cameras or security cameras that might have picked up Donnelly. I'm going to Campbell's office in … seven minutes," Deal said looking at his watch. "I want answers to those questions before I leave here."

Deal picked up his phone and dialed the FBI director's number. Deal explained the situation. The director assured Deal he would get a sweep underway of all law enforcement within two hundred miles, but both men knew chances were slim they could snare Donnelly that way. Too much time had passed. They didn't have a vehicle description or know in which direction to turn. Without more information they simply couldn't put together a tactical plan. Their only lead had just evaporated.

FORTY

Michael King gave Zach a conspiratorial grin. "Why not just go look for the car? They don't know me from Adam's housecat. You stayed in the truck, so the skinheads or whatever they are, probably wouldn't recognize you, and they sure wouldn't know my car," Michael said. "Anyway, you said you should probably do something, but the police wouldn't believe you. Let's find them something to believe."

"I don't know. Sounds kinda crazy to me. Those guys were real badasses. The kind you don't screw with," Zach said.

"We aren't going to mess with them. Just see if we can find them and see if they really are after some guy. If they are, we call the police. Come on! Tell you what. Let's get Bubba to go along. He can ride in the front. You can stay well out of sight in back. We probably won't be able to find them anyway," Michael argued.

"Well, OK. I'd feel better if Bubba comes along. He knows rednecks better than we do," Zach agreed reluctantly.

Michael called Bubba on his cell and, as usual, he was up for anything. Bubba came down to Michael's room and the three worked out a simple plan to get Zach out of the house without anyone seeing him. Zach didn't want Jimbo finding out he left with Michael and Bubba and suspecting that he spilled his guts about their ride to the 8-Ball.

Michael called Bubba's cell while they were all still in the room and then left and walked down the hall by himself. He reported back to Bubba that coast was clear and Bubba and Zach followed. They leapfrogged like this out of the frat house and into Michael's car. Nobody saw them together and nobody saw them leave, at least as far as they knew.

Michael drove out of the lot, down University to McFarland Boulevard, and turned right in the direction of the interstate. On their way, Zach described the unusual meeting between Jimbo, the rough character in the bright green Challenger, and Jimbo's threats afterward.

"Aw, hell," Bubba said. "I knew Jimbo could be an idiot, but this really beats all. No doubt about it, he's mixed up in something he shouldn't be, but I don't understand what he's doing ordering some Nazi rednecks to kidnap some poor guy. That just don't make sense. And why did he choose you to drive him there? I mean he's got a lot better friends in the house. There must be a reason."

"The only thing I can think of is that I owed him big because of the elections. Maybe he thought he could order me around and that I'd keep quiet about it," Zach answered.

"Now that sounds 'bout right to me," Bubba said. "I never did understand how a half-wit like Jimbo got to be such a big shot. He gives out orders like he's the godfather or something, just expecting everyone to jump when he says. Maybe he's part of a bigger thing, you know, maybe somebody higher up told him to do this thing. Maybe his family. You said Jimbo got all scared after the fact, right? Sounds to me like his butt's on the line about this deal gettin' done. Yep, Jimbo used you, my little friend," pointing at Zach in the back seat, "because he thought you were going to be part of that deal, whatever it is."

"You could be right, Bubba. But right now let's see if these guys are still around. Keep your eyes out for a bright green Dodge Challenger. Probably a Hellcat from the description Zach gave of them burning out of the truck stop. It won't be hard to spot," Michael declared.

"Where do you think we should go?" Bubba asked.

"I thought we'd cruise the hotels around the interstate. If they are looking for someone near the highway, that seems like a logical place to look," Michael said.

"And what are you sayin' we oughta do if we lay eyes on this crew?" Bubba asked.

Zach answered from the back seat. "Nothing! Just watch and maybe call the cops. I'm telling you, these guys don't play."

"Yeah, well, I seen lots a bad dudes at home," Bubba said. "Most are just poor rednecks with nothin' better to do than shoot off their mouths and act like idiots. Sometimes it's black guys who think they're gangbangers like in the big city. Maybe that's what we got here. A bunch of backwoods rednecks hired to do some job."

"I don't think so. The one guy I saw with Jimbo moved like he had military training. Like I told you, he had Jimbo face down on the car and in an arm lock like that!" Zach said snapping his fingers. "No, this guy was cool and confident. He didn't look backwoods to me at all."

"Keep your eyes open, we're coming up on a few hotels. Do you think we should drive around them?" Michael asked.

"No. These right here are too far down. I really think they were talking about an exit or two back toward Birmingham from here," Zach said.

"OK. We'll go north for two exits and get off there. I think there's some hotels and restaurants up there," Michael replied.

Michael swung the Mustang onto the ramp and gunned the engine. The 351-Cleveland V-8 roared, propelling the car forward and pushing the passengers back into their seats. Bubba had ridden in Michael's car several times, but he didn't remember it having this kind of power.

"You build this engine over the summer Michael? She feels a lot faster than last year," Bubba asked.

"Yeah, me and my dad upgraded the cam and changed out the carb to a bigger Holley. Not bad huh?" Michael said flooring the gas.

"Whooooo! Push that pedal boy! Let's go find us some bad guys!"

FORTY-ONE

"Have we got anything?" Deal asked his technical team. "Any video at all?"

"No, sir, sorry. This place just doesn't have video coverage anywhere. All we have is shots from our own cameras, and they were all pointed at the office building. Not away from it. Once Campbell drove outside our video perimeter, we lost him," the lead technical agent told Deal.

"OK, I guess it was a long shot anyway that this hick town would have climbed into the twenty-first century. I'm going to Campbell's office. Have teams Red and Blue sweep out to about forty miles then call them back in. I was gambling we'd get a lead and have a team close by, but it didn't pay off. Monitor my interview from here, act on your own authority if Campbell gives us anything," Deal ordered.

It was only a short drive to Campbell's office and Drew wasn't there yet. Deal used the time to review their camera placement and surveillance tactics. He satisfied himself that their plan had been sound. Donnelly was smart, no doubt about that. He managed to get into Tuscaloosa, meet with Drew Campbell, and disappear again, practically right under his nose. Deal vowed that wouldn't happen again.

A few minutes later, Campbell arrived. He got out of the car and looked around. He didn't immediately see

Deal, although he saw another car already there before he turned into the parking lot. Drew didn't like the thought of being surprised in the dark twice in one night.

Deal stepped into a pool of light. "Thanks for meeting me like this. We need to talk," he said moving toward the front door of the office building without offering to shake hands.

Drew fished in his pocket for his keys and followed Deal to the front door. After stepping inside and turning off the security system, Drew invited Deal back into the conference room.

Deal went in, but remained standing. "What happened?" he asked Drew.

"I told you what happened," Drew said. "Do you want to hear it again?"

Deal nodded, so Drew described yet again how he had been surprised in the YMCA parking lot earlier that night by Rick Donnelly.

"We went inside, and we had a brief meeting. I told him about your unexpected visit here and I advised him to get a criminal defense lawyer and turn himself in. He wanted a package of documents he gave me the night we met. I told him they were missing; and, that I couldn't represent him anymore. I also advised him not to tell me anything else he didn't want the FBI to know and he didn't. I asked him about sending back his retainer and he just said, 'keep it.' He walked out, and that was it," Drew explained.

"He said nothing about where he was going, or where he had been?" Deal asked.

"No," Drew replied. "Not a word."

"You said he approached you in the parking lot, did you see what kind of vehicle he was driving?"

"Again, like I told you, no," Drew answered. "I stayed inside the building for ten or fifteen minutes. He was clearly upset, and after what you told me, I didn't know what he might do or be capable of doing." Deal's pointed and accusatory sounding questioning didn't sit well with Drew and he let his irritation show in his voice.

"After what we discussed, I would think you might at least have tried to see what kind of car he was in," Deal shot back.

"Think whatever you like Agent Deal. But I have a family and I'm not going to play secret agent. I'll answer your questions, but don't start acting like any of this is my fault, because it's just not. I'm tired and won't play games with you if you don't play games with me," Drew responded.

"OK. OK. Let me ask you this. What package of documents are you talking about? You didn't mention this to me before."

"In point of fact, I am, and was, under no obligation to tell you anything at all. You simply showed up at my office one day with a fantastic story of espionage, theft, and murder. You wanted me to break my oath and reveal privileged information. I wouldn't be much of a lawyer if I had done that. So the package of documents, which by the way is now missing, was my client's business and that made it mine to protect," Drew responded in kind and not backing down.

"Well, don't be too sure, Mr. Campbell. Obstruction of justice is a serious charge. Those documents were important. Did you see what was in them or make a copy for any reason?"

"No. I never opened the package. It was locked in my safe the day after Donnelly and I had dinner. I only found out they were missing a day or two ago. Now it's my turn to ask a question, Agent Deal. How do you know they were important? Nobody even knows the combination to that safe except my partner and me and when I opened the safe everything else was still in place. Only Donnelly's documents, which I personally placed carefully on top of the others, were missing. You wouldn't have any information concerning that, do you? Breaking and entering is also a serious charge," Rick challenged.

"Lawyers, for crying out loud!" Deal exclaimed. "This is getting us no place. I need to find Donnelly. Everything else comes second. If you know anything about Donnelly's whereabouts, you need to tell me now. I've explained what this means to the country so I expect you to cooperate. If I find out you've been lying about anything, I'll be back," Deal threatened.

"I have cooperated, to the fullest extent of the law," Drew responded.

"I sincerely hope so, for your sake. You don't want to see me again. Next time I'll have a warrant," Deal said.

Not letting Deal have the satisfaction of believing he was intimidated, Drew tossed back his own threat. "That's fine with me. But if I find out you've conducted any kind of search or seizure here *without* a warrant, you'll see me again too."

Yeah, sure. Good luck with that buddy, Deal thought as he walked out of the conference room throwing a backhanded wave over his shoulder. *I'll be listening.*

FORTY-TWO

After leaving the YMCA building, Rick turned away from the front door, staying in the shadows. His senses tuned to high alert, Rick kept moved quickly toward his truck, knowing that if the FBI followed Drew and him here, he would be arrested in the next few moments. And there wasn't a thing he could do about it.

But nothing happened. He needed to get out of town and his old truck was the only option. Drew hadn't followed him out of the building, and Rick saw that his ex-lawyer wasn't watching from the door. Plus, Drew hadn't seen him park, he was sure of that. He waited nervously in the shadows for a few moments until a couple came out of the building together. Happily kidding each other about the racket ball game they just lost to another couple, they didn't see Drew walk casually past them and get in his vehicle. As the couple pulled out of their parking space, Rick followed suit, following them out of the far exit. Rick calculated that anyone seeing two vehicles leaving at the same time would at least have some doubt about which one he was in. As it turned out, Rick drove straight out of town completely unmolested, but his hands didn't stop shaking for another twenty minutes.

Rick felt like he was seven years old again, being chased by neighborhood bullies through the dusty streets of his hometown. Back then, Rick counted upon his intellect to avoid getting beat up. Using cunning, guile, and misdirection, Rick would lose his pursuers almost every time and make it safely back to the security of his grandmother's house. He knew the FBI might be close behind, so he took an unlikely path out of Tuscaloosa.

Rick needed to get to Austin, Texas, where Dave Knox and The Klass would keep him safe. But Austin lay 750 miles to the southwest. The busy interstate from Birmingham passed Tuscaloosa and continued on a southwesterly path into Mississippi, but Rick needed to avoid the interstates. He figured that anyone searching for him would have to assume he would take the fastest route possible and concentrate resources along and around the interstate system. So, he headed north instead, crossing the Black Warrior River and into the town of Northport. After driving through the little town's back streets, he turned left, passing the Tuscaloosa airport. Rick drove carefully and well within the speed limit down a two-lane state highway, driving through towns with the quaint names of Coker, Buhl, and Elrod, finally turning west again just before the town of Gordo.

After driving for an hour and swallowing a generous dose of paranoia, Rick at last decided he had successfully eluded capture by the FBI "bullies." In order to stay completely off the grid, he determined to forgo buying another cell phone. He also didn't want to waste any more time or risk that the authorities would be checking anyplace he might stop to get some rest, so Rick decided to drive through the night. The fastest route between west Alabama and Austin, Texas, would have taken over twelve hours. Rick's planned route along the back roads of Alabama, Mississippi, Louisiana, and Texas would take over eighteen. He needed a very large cup of coffee.

FORTY-THREE

J.P. looked at Skeeter from the driver's seat of his Challenger. They had parked at a Ruby Tuesday restaurant just across the street from the Hillmont Inn. Skeeter continued with his explanation about how to literally smoke their quarry, Rick Donnelly, out of the hotel.

"It won't take a real big fire to set off the fire alarm and cause an evacuation. Perhaps a trash can in one of the restrooms. Or, we can set a grease fire in the kitchen they use to prepare breakfast. Nobody will be in there this time of night."

"Are you serious?" J.P. said. "Why don't we just go in there and ask for him or his room number or something?"

"Because they won't give it to you. If you know a guest's name they will ring his room for you. But the chances are zero that if Donnelly is staying over there, he checked in under his own name. As I understand the situation, time is short. Get Mikey to walk inside and make his way to the kitchen. Have him put some oil in a big pan, turn on the stove, and walk out again. The delay in getting the oil to burn will give him time to exit. And, if someone happens into the kitchen before ignition, they will assume someone was trying to cook something and walked away. Simple," Skeeter explained.

"Why Mikey? Why not me or Dog?" J.P. asked.

"Because he looks the least like a mass murderer," Skeeter said.

"Oh, don't try kissing my ass with compliments, you bug-eyed insect. OK, let's make it happen. We'll have to move fast once the alarm goes off. You and I will walk over from this position like we just want to see what's going on. Dog and Gina can do the same from around back," J.P. suggested.

"Yes. Sound tactics. Have them ask any unattached man over about twenty-five if they know Rick Donnelly. Each reaction will tell us everything we need to know. Whoever finds him, just put a gun to his back and walk back to the nearest vehicle. I estimate the building will empty within three minutes of the alarm sounding and the fire department will arrive no more than four minutes after that given the proximity of the nearest station. We should be pre-positioned as near as possible but far enough away to avoid suspicion," Skeeter advised.

J.P. called Dog on his cell and explained the plan. Mikey agreed to infiltrate the hotel.

Five minutes after J.P. green-lighted the plan, Mikey walked through the front entrance of the hotel. It was nicer than he expected, a comfortable looking seating area to the right contained couches, armchairs, and multiple restaurant style tables. The front desk was straight ahead. A lone clerk held a phone against one ear as she busily typed at a computer. She didn't even notice him.

Mikey wasted no time strolling into the lounge area. He easily located the breakfast area in a separate room near the back. Entering through its open doorway, he found empty tables against every wall that would hold all the items the hotel offered as its free breakfast. But now, it was deserted. A single door marked "Employees Only" clearly led to the kitchen at the other end. He stopped and leaned against the wall for ten seconds, listening for any sound from inside. After hearing nothing, he tried the door. It was locked.

Looking at the lock again, Mikey grinned to himself. This lock might keep out curious guests or some kids, but otherwise it was a joke. He pulled a switchblade out of his back pocket, snapped out the blade and inserted it between the door and the jam. It took him no more than two seconds to defeat the lock and open the door. He quickly slid inside and closed the door behind him. Sure enough, behind the door was a small but neatly laid out professional-style kitchen. It was obvious that the kitchen saw only light use. Probably just to cook eggs, bacon, sausage, and the like for the breakfast bar. Mikey lost no time doing his own cooking.

Choosing a large stainless steal frying pan from the rack above his head, he placed it on the gas stove and began searching for cooking oil. He found it in a large pantry at the far end of the kitchen. Several bottles of vegetable oil stood on the top shelf. Taking one down, he headed back to the stove.

Now he had to decide how much oil to use. More oil would take longer to heat up, but would cause a bigger fire. Less would catch faster, but would not make very impressive flames. He ended up filling the large pan over half full, relying on the fast and intense heat of the gas cook top to speed things up. Now he added his own touch. Mikey hung several dry dishtowels above the pan. These would catch on fire, drop to the floor and make the fire appear larger, even if it would be no more dangerous. Silently congratulating himself on this little innovation, Mikey turned the gas on under the pan to "Max" and turned to leave. Just as he was about to go out the door he heard another door open at the end of a hallway that led into the back of the kitchen.

Mikey froze, listening for footsteps. He knew he couldn't be caught in the employee area and he had no way to bluff his way out. Even if he snuck out now, whoever this was would find the oil heating up and ruin the plan.

The footsteps continued slowly toward the kitchen, so Mikey moved again, silently concealing himself against a side wall at the end of the hall. Then someone called, "Rosa? Estas aqui? Are you here?" Just then a short dark figure emerged from the hall walking right past Mikey. The Latino arrived at the hotel's service entrance a few minutes earlier to give Rosa, one of the hotel laundry staff a ride home. When she wasn't at the door, he decided to look for her inside.

The man saw and smelled the oil filled pan just beginning to smoke on the stove. "Que es esto? What is this?"

Mikey had only one second to make a decision before the man turned around. He acted. Mikey took two quick steps forward and wrapped his left arm around the man's neck, sliding his right arm behind the neck and grabbing his left upper arm putting his target into a classic choke hold. This should have dropped the man almost immediately, but his angle was imperfect. While Mikey stood over six feet two inches tall, his opponent was a good seven or eight inches shorter and built like a tank. Mikey never fought anyone so compact and muscular. The short Latino grabbed at Mikey's arm still locked around his neck and pulled down with all his might. Mikey tried to lift the man up and back to put pressure on the carotid artery, stopping blood flow to the brain and choking him out. But this was easier said than done. He didn't have the leverage to lift the man off his feet. The two men were deadlocked and neither could gain an advantage. Then, Mikey's training in hand-to-hand combat kicked in. Since he couldn't pull the man backward, Mikey suddenly stopped trying.

The tough Latino's immense effort to pull forward and down now worked against him. He tried to take one step forward, but lost his balance falling face first with Mikey's arms still locked around his neck. The awkward angle of the impact with the floor combined with Mikey's weight on his back snapped his neck. The tough Latino's body went completely limp. Mikey clearly heard the cervical vertebrae shatter and he knew immediately the man was dead.

Mikey got up and looked around, making sure they were alone. The fight didn't last fifteen seconds, but he saw the oil was already throwing off faint tendrils of smoke. Mikey didn't give the man's life a second thought, but a dead body would be a problem. He couldn't very well carry this guy outside. So Mikey moved quickly back to the pantry. After a moment, he found several bottles of lamp fuel, kerosene. The hotel probably used this stuff in the warming tables or maybe for its tiki torches around the pool. Mikey unscrewed the tops on two bottles and doused the entire kitchen. Now he had no choice. He had to leave.

Shaken and sweating from the mortal struggle, Mikey smoothed his clothing and his hair, took two deep breaths, and noiselessly left the kitchen. His hands were shaking from the adrenaline jolt delivered during the confrontation, so he stuck them in the pockets of his jeans. Keeping his head down and his face away from the direction of the front desk, he walked smoothly out the front door, around the building and back to Dog's truck.

J.P. and Skeeter saw Mikey enter and leave the building. They watched closely for any sign of trouble, but noted nothing. J.P. called Dog when they saw Mikey was back.

"How'd it go?" J.P. asked Dog. "Any problems?"

"Mikey says it's all good. The nice hotel guests will be scurrying out the doors any minute," Dog reported.

"OK, move toward the building as soon as there's any activity," J.P. ordered. "You know what to do. And take Gina, having a girl along will make you look more legit."

Back in the safety of Dog's truck, Mikey considered whether to tell J.P. that, yeah, he had a problem during his little adventure. But he rationalized that now was not the time. They had more work to do and he didn't want to complicate the operation at this point.

Gina, who was sitting between Dog and Mikey in the front seat, looked at Mikey and wrinkled her nose. "You smell weird," she said.

"Yeah, well I think they've been cooking a little Mexican in there," Mikey responded with a smile.

FORTY-FOUR

"Hold it, hold it!" Bubba suddenly blurted out pointing at something. "Is that it?"

"Where?" Michael asked as he stepped on the brakes.

"Over there, at the edge of Ruby Tuesday's parking lot! Kinda in the shadows between the lights. Right there!" Bubba answered, excitedly jabbing his finger at the right front window.

Zach pulled himself up between the front bucket seats and peered at where Bubba was pointing. "Yeah, I think that's it! Pull in here, quick!" he said. "I don't want to drive by them."

Michael had slowed just enough so he could manage a fast left into the McDonald's next door to the restaurant where the bright green Challenger sat pointed directly at the hotel across the street.

"Well I'll be damned! Zach was right … for a change," Bubba mocked. "What do we do now?"

"Watch. I think I see two people in there, but I can't be sure. What do you think?" Michael asked his friends.

"I can't tell either," Zach replied.

"I got somethin' that just might help," Bubba said reaching down between his legs. "My daddy gave me these."

"No thanks Bubba, anything down there your daddy gave you, you can just keep covered!" Michael joked.

"Oooo, you're reeeeal funny!" Bubba retorted. "I mean these."

Bubba pulled a pair of compact binoculars up to his eyes. He scanned the car for a moment and handed them to Zach.

"Two guys for sure," Bubba reported. "Are those the skinheads?"

Zach studied the car for another minute. "I can't tell, too dark. But if that ain't the same car, it's an exact match to the one I saw. Geez Bubba, these are nice, like high def."

"German optical precision by Zeiss," explained Bubba, pronouncing the manufacturer as "Zees."

Michael said, "OK then, we have the same car, sitting across the street from a hotel with two guys inside. Looks like Zach heard right. Let's just see what they do next, maybe they're looking for that Donny guy. We're parked at an angle and behind them, I doubt they'll notice us, especially if they're fixated on the hotel."

"Man, I'm hungry!" Bubba said. "How 'bout I go on in and get us some Big Macs or somethin'?"

"Damn, Bubba, we just ate a while ago! You musta had three plates of spaghetti. Chill out for now," Michael said.

Bubba gave Michael a baleful look. "You know them eye-talian noodles never fill me up. But, OK, I don't want to miss anything anyway." Bubba sat back in his seat crossing his arms across his broad chest. "But if this turns out to be a false alarm, y'all are ordering me a large pizza when we get back."

Michael and Zach wouldn't be buying him a pizza.

FORTY-FIVE

J.P. and Skeeter watched and waited; but J.P. was getting concerned. It seemed like a long time since Mikey came out of the hotel, yet the still and peaceful scene before him hadn't changed. If Mikey didn't do this right they'd have to come up with another plan altogether. Mikey got lucky ducking in and out without raising any apparent suspicion and J.P. didn't want to push their luck by having to go back in.

He was about to ask Skeeter to think up an alternative strategy when a red light on the side of the hotel began flashing. Moments later, they heard an alarm. If they could hear it clearly from this far away, it must have been ear piercing inside. Skeeter got excited. "See, just like I said!"

Now smoke began rising from the front entrance and drifted over the top of the building in J.P. and Skeeter's direction. "Let's go! Easy. Like we just want to see what's going on."

Skeeter bounded out of the car and looked like he was going to start running. J.P. grabbed him by the collar. "I said easy!" Skeeter didn't resist.

"Yeah, sorry. This is just so cool!" Skeeter said as excited as a kid on Christmas morning.

The pair jogged slowly across the street as the parking lot surrounding the building began to fill with occupants of the hotel. Some were fully dressed, others wore pajamas while a few stood uncomfortably wrapped only in towels. Hotel staff was already approaching the displaced guests trying to check off room occupants who made it outside.

While J.P. and Skeeter slowly walked around the outside of the ever-growing mass of evacuees, Dog and Gina approached the hotel from the opposite direction. They witnessed smoke now pouring out of the open doors. As they got closer, they heard a crash from the direction of the one-story extension built on the side of the five story main building. Within seconds, flame exploded out of its collapsed roof. Several smaller explosions and pops could be heard from within the heart of the inferno.

"Ooooo! Mikey's grease fire really took off! He did good!" Gina squealed with delight.

"That ain't no grease fire, girl. I don't know what else he done, but ain't no pan of grease did that! Come on and start looking for guys standing around alone. Just walk up and say somethin' like 'Mr. Donnelly?' We'll know when it's him. I'll be right behind you, stick my nice little Walther in his ribs, and walk him away. Got it?"

"No problemo!" Gina enthusiastically agreed, walking quickly toward the crowd milling around outside.

J.P. and Skeeter had the same plan. Skeeter, whose size and appearance made him far less threatening than J.P., would approach each potential target with J.P. close behind. J.P. carried a Ruger SP 357 Magnum. Its 2.25

inch barrel and powerful magnum ammunition made it one of the most popular concealed-carry revolvers. J.P. preferred a revolver because they didn't eject shell casings all over the place and because it looked ridiculously fearsome.

The two teams started searching. But, their plan had not considered the possibility that the hotel guests would stay so close together after emerging from the hotel. Families stood or sat together holding each other, comforting crying children and continuously checking on each other. Off to one side two adult women had a group of ten- or twelve-year-old girls gathered together. One of the women counted each girl over and over; never completely satisfied she had counted correctly. There were many couples, young and old, all with their arms wrapped around each other. Both teams had more trouble than expected just identifying single white men to confront.

The evacuated guests stood wide-eyed and staring back at the hotel. Now flames could be seen in the lobby area where the club chairs blazed brightly. Within just a few minutes, the flames would defeat the fire suppression system and fire-retardant walls and ceilings. If left unchecked, it would climb floor by floor eventually devouring the entire structure from the inside out.

J.P. now moved a little faster. The fire department and police would be at the scene within minutes. Once the police arrived, it would be impossible to successfully abduct and secure their target.

Skeeter sidled up to a short rotund balding man with glasses. He wore a pair of stripped pajama pants but his torso was wrapped only in a towel.

"Excuse me," Skeeter said walking up to the bald man's side. "Mr. Donnelly?"

The bald man looked at Skeeter, his eyes still wide with fright. It took a moment for him to realize someone had spoken to him. "Are you talking to me?"

"Yes, I'm sorry. Are you Mr. Donnelly by any chance?" Skeeter asked.

"Uh no, I don't know any Donnelly," the man said and then turned back to the fire, lost in his own thoughts.

Skeeter approached two other men who seemed to be alone. Each reacted much like the fat bald towel-guy. Sirens could now be heard approaching quickly. The mission was running out of time fast. Skeeter moved a little faster but could only locate one other possibility, but without success.

J.P. stayed behind Skeeter making sure he didn't miss anyone. With a glance over his shoulder, J.P. saw multiple red flashing lights through the trees. Looking in the opposite direction, he saw two police vehicles flying down the exit ramp of the interstate. If they had no luck in the next twenty seconds they would have to abort.

Skeeter turned back to J.P. and said, "Dog and Gina are only twenty feet away. If he were here, we would have found him. I must conclude that he isn't here and that we should exit."

J.P. grudgingly nodded. He caught Dog's eye, and pointed at the fast approaching police. When Dog looked back, J.P. ran his index finger across his throat, signaling an end to the mission.

Once back inside the car, Skeeter analyzed the situation, "If Donnelly was in that hotel, we would have found him. I'm certain of it. The plan was sound and the execution within expected parameters."

"What do you mean, 'expected parameters'?" J.P. asked.

"I mean the execution of the plan, the way it was performed, was good but not perfect," Skeeter said, continuing with his analysis. "The intensity of the fire was greater than necessary. A chance exists that someone, perhaps even Donnelly, was overcome by smoke or flame and didn't make it out of the building. We have no way to know until fire officials report injuries or deaths. However, I believe less than a two percent chance exists that this is the reason for our lack of success."

"You mean failure, don't you?" J.P. snarled between clenched teeth.

Skeeter looked at how J.P.'s hands clenched the steering wheel and the tendons of his forearms looked like steel bands stretched taught under the skin.

Skeeter wisely replied, "No, failure would connote fault on our part. Lack of success means our actions were based on faulty information."

"Well I don't like either one. Jimbo owes me an explanation."

FORTY-SIX

"What's that?" Zach asked from the backseat.

"What's what?" Bubba responded.

"That blinking red light on the side of the hotel. It just came on a second ago," Zach said excitedly.

"Oh, man! I know what that is! It's a fire signal. It's tripped by the fire alarm and emits that light to warn people away and mark the building for the fire department. Wait," Bubba said, "do you hear that? The interior fire alarm is activated. There's a real fire over there!"

"Hey! Hey!" Michael shouted. "Look there, quick, the guys in the Challenger got out. Zach, take the binoculars, is that the same guy?"

"I don't need them. No doubt at all, that's the skinhead. What did I tell you, is this weird or what?" Zach exclaimed. Then he asked, "What should we do?"

"You do nothing at all. Stay here and don't even get out of the car. We don't know what these guys are up to and we can't risk them recognizing you," Michael said.

"Yeah, that strikes me as a very bad idea, too," Zach said.

"Why don't we just stroll over there like a couple of gawkers and see what we can see Michael? Maybe if we get closer, we can get a clue about what these guys are doing and what Jimbo's into," Bubba suggested.

"Well we don't know them, so I bet they wouldn't know us. Look!" Michael said suddenly pointing.

They could see the glow of flames in the back of the building getting brighter while huge plumes of smoke rose up and over the hotel, the flames and lights from the streetlamps giving it a hellish red and yellow glow.

"Let's go!" Bubba said.

"OK, but we stay well clear. No heroics, Bubba. We have no idea what they're doing or why. And, we don't know if they're armed or not. Got it?" Michael said in a near-commanding tone.

"Yes, sir, Sarge," Bubba said throwing a left-hand salute. "We're wasting time."

Bubba and Michael got out of the Mustang, leaving Zach in the back seat. They ran across the street but slowed once they got to the other side. They could still see the skinhead and the little geek. Bubba pretended to watch the fire while Michael kept his eye on the pair from the Challenger.

Their movements indicated to Michael that they weren't just curious about the fire. In fact, they seemed disinterested in the spectacle developing nearby, and focused instead on the people running out of the hotel and gathering on the far side of the parking lot. Like Zach said, they were looking for someone.

Keeping up their rubbernecking act, Bubba and Zach kept their distance, but stayed close enough to see what the skinhead and his smaller partner were doing. Michael was watching when the short, thin, and disheveled skinhead approached a lone man. They spoke for a moment before the smaller man moved away. Michael and Bubba watched this same scene play out several more times. The entire time the geeky skinhead was speaking to various hotel guests, the muscular one remained close but inconspicuous. Then they heard sirens.

Almost immediately Michael watched as the obvious leader spoke into his partner's ear, pointed at approaching police and made a signal to a third person in the crowd. Turning around, they began walking in Michael and Bubba's direction.

Michael and Bubba needed to disappear. As Bubba watched the fire, Michael placed his hand on Bubba's shoulder and gently pushed him forward into the cluster of displaced guests and curious onlookers. He left his hand on Bubba shoulder, leaning on him as if he needed comforting. Realizing what Michael was doing, Bubba put his arm around Michael and pulled him close.

Michael saw the two skinheads pass behind them without breaking stride.

"Alright big boy, you can remove you huge mitt from me now. They're leaving," Michael said.

"I don't know," Bubba joked, not looking down at Michael. "You're kinda soft and squishy like a girl and you did bring me along because I'm big and strong."

Michael ducked from under Bubba's massive arm. "Uck! You could have put on deodorant at least. They left. Let's get back to the car."

"Gee, I'm sorry honey, short notice," Bubba threw back at Michael.

As they walked back Bubba said, "Hey, I noticed something about the skinhead I bet you didn't. He was carrying."

"Great, just great," Michael said sarcastically. "We have to find out what's going on here, Bubba. Whatever Jimbo's got Zach involved in, it ain't good. Those guys were definitely hunting for someone in particular, like a pack of wolves. Whoever they are and whatever they're up to, it's serious, deadly serious. Let's get back to the house."

FORTY-SEVEN

Michael wheeled out of the McDonald's and pointed the car back toward campus. All three occupants rode in silence for a few minutes lost in their own thoughts. Bubba finally broke the stressful atmosphere.

"I been thinking on it, and I don't think we can call the police about this. I mean, what do we have? A college kid who heard a strange conversation and then the three of us tracking down these jokers? You know, they didn't even do anything illegal. They seemed to be searching for someone, but that's all we know. The cops would blow us off. And, they'd be right," Bubba said, analyzing their situation.

Reacting to Bubba's comments Zach blurted, "But they had guns! And I know what I heard, they were trying to find this Donny and grab him. Crap, I don't know. What do you think Michael? You haven't said anything."

Michael kept his eyes on the road, while his mind turned over the events of the night. Reaching a conclusion, he voiced his thoughts. "All I know for sure right now is that whatever Jimbo and the skinheads are into is no good. No good at all. I don't like the fact that Zach is so close to this thing. And I know for a fact we're in over our heads. Zach, what do you think about me calling my dad and asking for a little advice? I'll keep you and Bubba out of it and say it's one of our frat brothers who might be mixed up with some bad guys, drug dealers or something."

"Yeah, OK, I admit it, I'm a little scared," Zach confessed. "But I absolutely don't want my father involved. He'd pull me out of school and make me join the Navy or Army for God's sake. Yeah, why not, give him a call when we get back."

"Sounds right to me," Bubba commented. "Your dad's a straight-up guy."

Michael thought about what he would and could tell his father. *He could say a friend of his is scared because he agreed to help someone sell prescription painkillers. The deal didn't happen like it was suppose to, maybe his "friend" couldn't come up with the promised drugs, or changed his mind. The prospective buyers threatened him, but now he doesn't want to go the police. What should he do? Something like that.*

Michael ran the story by Bubba and Zach. They approved. Michael didn't want to lie to his father but Zach needed some advice. And they couldn't risk it getting back to Mr. Self.

The car became quiet again as they drove up McFarland Boulevard. Lights from fast food joints, strip malls, and car lots lit the road and cast a flickering yellow-orange glow across the unsmiling faces of the three fraternity brothers.

Without warning, Bubba pointed ahead and yelled, "There!"

Startled by Bubba's sudden outburst, Michael said, "What? Where?"

Zach's head appeared between the seats, his eyes wide trying to see what Bubba pointed at.

"There!" Bubba said again. "Wendy's! They're open late! I need a burger!"

FORTY-EIGHT

J.P. called Jimbo's cell phone after The Boys' unsuccessful attempt to locate Rick Donnelly. J.P. explained how they forced the guests out of the hotel and then searched for their target among the evacuated guests. J.P. was pissed. He accused Jimbo of giving them the wrong location and blamed him for the failure of the mission.

"Now hold on J.P. I just passed on the location I was given. How was I to know it wasn't right?" Jimbo responded, defending himself from the unwarranted accusation.

"Fine. Then I want to talk to these people," J.P. said. "We can still get this done."

"That ain't going to happen J.P. and you know it," Jimbo said. "That info came from way up somewhere and I only talked to anyone at all because Hunter wasn't here. I gotta report and then it's out of my hands."

"If you're going to report, I ought to be the one to talk to them. I'm on my way there," J.P. pronounced.

"No! We can't be connected, you know that don't… "

"I'll stay in the lot. Come down or I'll come up there. You know I will, so quit screwing around with me." J.P. abruptly ended the call.

"Aw shee-ut," Jimbo said to himself. He grabbed his phone and headed downstairs. It was late and the halls of the frat house were all but deserted. As he made his way outside Jimbo watched J.P. wheel into the space farthest from the house. Paranoid someone would see him, Jimbo moved as quickly as he could out of the light from the front porch, around several cars and out to where J.P. parked his car. Jimbo went directly to the driver's side. J.P. already had the window down.

"OK, make the call," J.P. said.

"Goddammit, J.P. I told you that's not how it's done. You really should get out of here. We can't be seen together," Jimbo said, almost pleading with him.

"That kid that drove you saw us together earlier. I'll tell you what, just get in and we'll drive around and report. If they got some more info for us, I want to hear it first hand and be ready to act," J.P. commanded.

Just as J.P. finished his sentence, Michael's car pulled into the lot. The headlights from his Mustang revealed the bright green Challenger with Jimbo leaning in the passenger window. Michael and Bubba saw Jimbo look up like a deer caught in their high beams.

"Zach, duck!" Michael said as soon as he saw the Challenger and Jimbo.

Zach was sitting in the dark back seat behind Michael. Michael's convertible had only a small triangular window for back seat passengers, but Zach threw himself down across the seat anyway. Michael saw Jimbo glower at him as they drove past. Thinking fast, Michael tossed Jimbo a small wave, just raising the fingers of his left hand off the wheel.

"Great!" Zach moaned. "If Jimbo finds me back here he'll think I betrayed him, which I did. I'm screwed!"

"Chill, and stay down in the seat. I don't think he saw you and he's not acting like anything is wrong," Michael explained as he watched Jimbo in his review mirror. "I'm pulling on down to the other end. Bubba and I will get out. I'll call you when it's OK to come in. Bubba, you act a little drunk. Give Jimbo a big 'ole hello or something."

"Gotcha," acknowledged Bubba.

After parking, he and Bubba got out and closed the doors. Michael locked the car while Bubba leaned drunkenly on the passenger side.

"Come on, buddy, I got to study," Michael said in a normal tone.

"Aw come on! We got time for a one and done!" Bubba blurted loudly enough for Jimbo to hear.

As they walked toward the front door, Bubba looked over toward Jimbo, raised one hand, and yelled in a mocking tone at Michael's expense, "Jimbo! Come on and get a brewski! This here baby wants to stuuuudddddyyyy!

Jimbo just glared at them and waved off Bubba's fake invitation.

"Well, aw-righty then, I'll just drink yours my own self!" Bubba replied with false hurt in his voice.

Michael and Bubba went on into the house and closed the door. They moved quickly up the stairs to

Bubba's room, where they could watch Jimbo from the window. They were just in time to see him get into the bright green car and drive away from campus toward downtown Tuscaloosa.

Michael quickly called Zach, who joined them in Bubba's room.

"Oh, man. Ain't no doubt Jimbo's up to something with Mr. Skinhead," Bubba said. "We just don't know what, at least for sure."

"Let's break up for tonight. I'll call my dad in the morning, it's too late now anyway. Zach, stay cool. We really don't know for sure what's going on anyway. We'll work it out tomorrow," Michael suggested.

Zach didn't sleep that night. His mind automatically conjured up multiple worst-case scenarios. None were really bad enough.

FORTY-NINE

"Who was that?" J.P. asked Jimbo as they left the fraternity house lot.

"Just a couple of frat brothers. The big drunk one, Bubba, is just a redneck from south Alabama. His daddy owns grocery stores or something. The driver's name is Michael King. A nobody. I don't think they're anything to worry about, except for the fact they saw me with this loud green car of yours. I told you not to come to the house. They probably won't think twice about it, but now I have to keep an eye on them," Jimbo sounded irritated and smelled like bourbon.

"Just make the call," J.P. growled. He was getting tired of Jimbo's whining.

Jimbo called Hunter, reluctantly. He kept his part of the conversation short, passing along that the mission had failed to locate the target. Hunter demanded an explanation and details. Jimbo relayed how he had given The Boys the relevant information and left it in their hands, per orders.

J.P. didn't like the way Jimbo seemed to be assigning blame to him and The Boys so he grabbed the phone away from Jimbo and said, "Listen, all we were given was a name and faulty information about his location. We didn't miss Donnelly for the simple reason he wasn't there. It was a hotel. If he had been inside we would have found him."

Hunter didn't know J.P.'s voice. "Who is this? Give the phone back to Jimbo now!" Hunter commanded.

"It's J.P. Jimbo here doesn't know anything. If you want to know what happened you have to talk to me," J.P. retorted.

"God almighty, J.P.! You're supposed to have as little contact as possible with us! What are you doing?" Hunter demanded.

"Just riding around. I'll return him safe and sound. Now listen up, if there's additional information I can use, get it now. I don't like loose ends and I'll bet The Doyens don't either. Do you have anything else on this guy?"

"No. Let Jimbo out wherever you are and go home. Now. I have calls to make. Do you understand me?" Hunter ordered.

"Yes, sir, boss!" J.P. said with sarcastic respect.

"One more thing, you didn't leave a mess behind while searching this hotel did you?" Hunter asked.

"Yeah, well, we sanitized the place real good. Not one speck of evidence left behind." J.P. said, reaching his hand over the seat to high-five Skeeter.

FIFTY

The next morning, Michael waited until he knew his father would be at work. Allen King made it a point to be at work by seven-thirty, even though the office didn't open until eight. So even before his first class, Michael dialed his father's office number. Allen didn't expect a call from Michael so early in the morning. While Michael called home regularly, he usually waited until the evening. Allen answered the phone and asked if everything was all right. Michael assured him it was and began by telling his father that he needed some advice to help out a friend who might be in some trouble.

"Sure," Allen said. "No problem. This 'friend' isn't actually you, is it?

"Nope, it's a frat brother. He promised some guys that he could get a supply of prescription meds and sell it to them," Michael explained uneasily.

"Is that right? You don't sound very convinced about that." Allen asked gently.

Michael never developed the ability to effectively lie to his father. He would immediately feel guilty about trying and would come clean. Today was no different.

"Dad, look, I'm sorry. That's not true at all. Can I start over?" Michael asked.

"Sure son. Why don't you do that. What's going on? If you're not in trouble, then who is?"

"It's Zach Dad. I really need your advice, but he doesn't want his father involved. You know how Mr. Self is. He'd overreact and assume Zach has done something wrong, and he hasn't. Can we make a deal not to tell him? It's important to Zach," Michael requested.

"No promises. If he's in trouble with the law or in real danger, then I'll have to go to his father. But, let me hear it and we'll see. That's the only deal I can make." Allen knew Michael was just looking out for Zach. But Zach was also like a member of his own family and he would put Zach's well being first, just as he would his own son's.

Michael knew his father would do whatever he thought best, but he also knew his father would be reasonable. They trusted each other, a relationship that Zach didn't have with his own father.

Michael spent the next five minutes explaining the events of last night, how Zach drove Jimbo to the 8-Ball, the part of the conversation he overheard, their search for the green Challenger, and the hotel fire. He also described how they saw Jimbo meeting with the same guys that they saw working the crowd at the fire scene when they got back to the frat house.

Allen listened without asking a single question. He wasn't pleased that Michael and Zach acted impulsively going out looking for the tough characters that this Jimbo met with; but he also understood their reluctance to go to the police. Allen didn't believe the police would have taken any action either. Michael and Zach just hadn't seen either Jimbo or his associates do anything wrong. Sure, their actions could be considered suspicious, but certainly not illegal. Yet, Michael's tone told him his son truly believed this situation needed attention of some kind.

Allen warned Michael not to take any more chances like he did last night. Allen dealt with the law every day. He worked with lawyers on lawsuits filed against people covered by his insurance company. But he didn't know anything about whether Zach might be an accomplice or have some liability if Jimbo or, as Michael described them, the "skinheads'" had actually engaged in some criminal activity.

"I understand your concern, but it seems to me there's a lot of missing pieces to the puzzle. Perhaps everything these guys did was perfectly innocent and you guys are being overly imaginative. Probably not though, from what you've told me. I don't think I have enough information to warrant a call to Zach's father, yet. Here's what I think you should do. Write down everything you guys did and saw last night while its fresh in your memory. I like to have notes about everything. Then I want you to go see a lawyer friend of mine. We've worked together and been friends for over fifteen years. He's a good guy and I trust him. Run this by him and see what he says. If he says go to the police, then do that. I'll give him a call, fill him in, and see if he's free today," Allen said.

"A lawyer? Really? Do you think it's that serious Dad?" Michael asked.

"That's just it, I don't know. Take Zach and Bubba with you. I guarantee he'll listen to you and help any way he can. Like I said, I trust him, he's the best lawyer I know and I know a lot of excellent attorneys. It's like going to a doctor when you think something's wrong, but don't know. The smart move is to get it checked out," Allen explained patiently.

"Yeah, I see your point. What's his name?" Michael inquired.

"Drew Campbell."

FIFTY-ONE

Allen King picked up the phone and dialed Drew Campbell. As usual, Drew greeted him warmly, and after exchanging the usual pleasantries, Allen told Drew about the call from his son Michael. Allen wasn't overly concerned. After all, fraternity boys getting into some trouble at college wasn't exactly rare. But Allen explained that Michael didn't normally get involved with any real trouble; and, he also wasn't prone to paranoia or embellishing the truth.

Drew readily agreed to meet with Michael, Zach, and anyone else they wanted to bring along. If nothing else, he promised to listen to their account of what happened and offer any advice he might have. Allen offered to pay Drew for his time, but Drew refused. They were friends and colleagues, and Allen's insurance company sent Drew all the work he could handle.

Allen King called his son back and suggested he and Zach go to Drew Campbell's office at three o'clock that afternoon.

"Thanks, Dad," Michael said. "I'm sorry to bother you with this, it's probably nothing at all, but I'd like to be sure. I hope it's not putting Mr. Campbell out too much."

Allen smiled on his end of the line. He was lucky to have a son with a head planted firmly on his shoulders. "Don't worry. Like I said, Drew's a good friend. Tell him everything and listen carefully to his advice. I trust his judgment and so should you."

At three that afternoon Michael, Zach, and Bubba sat in the waiting area of Campbell & Hamner, P.C. The large and overly exuberant secretary, Tracy, fussed over them, which only increased in intensity after she found out Michael was Allen King's son. She insisted that she get them all a Coke and bustled off down the hall. A minute or two later she was back, a little breathless, pressing three cans against her substantial bosom with one hand and carrying a plate of cookies in the other.

"Come on into the conference room gentlemen! Drew's on a call, but he'll be right in. Can I get you anything else? I've got a new bag of pretzels in my desk if y'all want something salty instead. I like salty snacks with Coke."

"Thank you, Ma'am, this is great," Zach said politely.

"I like pretzels," Bubba said, smiling at Tracy.

"Now I just thought you might," Tracy said beaming back at Bubba. She turned and left in a veritable whirlwind of flying hair and jiggling body parts.

"I never been to see a lawyer before," Bubba said. "Pretty dang nice place if you ask me."

Tracy reappeared a moment later with a new bag of miniature pretzels. Drew followed right behind her.

"Thanks, Tracy. Please hold my calls for a little while," Drew requested as Tracy placed the pretzel bag in front of Bubba.

"Yes, sir. Let me know if you need anything," she said as she left, closing the glass doors behind her.

Drew introduced himself, shaking hands with each of the boys in turn. He then motioned them to have a seat and put a legal pad and pen on the conference table.

Turning to Michael he said, "Michael, I've known your dad for a long time. It's nice to get to meet you finally. I've seen many pictures of you and your brother growing up and your dad has good things to say about you."

"Thank you Mr. Campbell, it's really nice of you to take your time to see us," Michael responded. Zach and Bubba echoed Michael's thanks.

"First, please don't call me Mr. Campbell. My name is Drew. So, let's get to it, your dad didn't have many details. I don't know if I will be able to help, but I sure can listen. So, who wants to fill me in?"

"I guess I better start," offered Zach. "I kinda got these guys involved."

"Alright then Zach, shoot," Drew said, picking up his pen preparing to make notes.

"Well, I was studying in my room last night after dinner. I think it was around eight o'clock. Jimbo shows up at my door and he'd been drinking," Zach began.

"Who's Jimbo?" Drew asked.

"Sorry, uh Jim Ewell. He's a senior and big deal in the frat and on campus. Anyway, he wants me to drive him out to the 8-Ball. So, since I owe him a favor, I drive him out there in his truck."

"What kind of favor did you owe him? And why did he want to go out there?" Drew asked.

"Well, see, Jimbo pulled some strings and got me on the ballot to run for The Tyros. He told me he had to meet some guys, no big deal, but he didn't want to drive because he wasn't sober."

"Go ahead. I'm just making notes because I'm old and forget things," Drew explained.

"Yeah, so we go around to the back of the 8-Ball's lot and Jimbo tells me to pull up near this car and pickup. Jimbo gets out, walks over, and starts talking to a real bad-looking guy that got out of the car, a bright green Challenger Wildcat."

"Pretty specific on the kind of car," Drew observed.

"Michael knew what it was as soon as I described it," Zach explained.

"That figures. I know Michael's dad is a real car guy, so I bet Michael is, too."

Zach continued. "Jimbo told me to stay in the truck, but I rolled the window down because this all looked weird and I wanted to figure out what he was doing. I could just make out some of what they were saying. Like I told Michael and Bubba, Jimbo told this skinhead guy that he, the skinhead, was supposed to grab someone named Donny or something like that and hold on to him."

"Like kidnapping him?" Drew asked looking up from his notes.

"Yeah. That's what I remember, it sounded like Jimbo was telling him to grab this Donny or Dondy or something like that," Zach said.

Drew Campbell stopped writing and looked up at Zach. *No, he thought, this really isn't possible. Is it?* Zach stopped talking when Drew looked up.

"You OK Mr. Campbell, uh, Drew?" Michael asked. He could clearly see Drew was stunned and that his hand holding his pen trembled, just a bit.

Not taking his eyes off Zach, Drew asked, "Could this Jimbo have said 'Donnelly'?"

"Yeah! That's it! Donnelly! Man, it's been on the tip of my tongue since last night! How did you know that?" Zach asked excitedly.

"I wish I didn't," Drew said almost to himself. "Uh, sorry. I'll get to how I know in a minute. Go ahead and tell me what happened after that."

Zach described how Jimbo got thrown around by the skinhead, how they returned to the frat house, and Jimbo's warnings about keeping his mouth shut.

"Then I called Michael because it was so dang strange and a little scary to tell you the truth," Zach said.

"Michael, how did you and Bubba get involved?" Drew asked.

Now Michael took over the story. "Zach called me, we talked about calling the police but decided we didn't have anything real to tell them. So we decided to get Bubba and go look around for that Challenger, you know, just to see if Jimbo had gotten Zach into something illegal. We figured the car would stick out like a sore thumb. Well, it did, and we found it near the Hillmont out by the interstate. We were actually there when the hotel caught on fire and we watched the skinhead guys going through the crowd asking questions. We didn't hear anything, but it looked like they might be looking for this, uh, Donnelly guy. But we can't say for sure. We watched them leave right as the fire trucks and police showed up. I guess that's about it."

"Can you add anything Bubba?" Drew asked.

"Not really. But I've dealt with people like that before. They're bad news. I just went along I guess for security," Bubba said. "Oh yeah, Michael forgot to tell you, when we got back to the house, the Challenger was in our parking lot and Jimbo was talking to these same guys again. I acted drunk, a superb performance by the way, so Michael and I could get back in the house without Jimbo getting suspicious. We left Zach in the car until Jimbo left again with the skinheads."

Drew had been taking notes, but now stopped and thought about the situation. This connection between Jimbo, the "skinheads," and Donnelly created a whole new dimension to an already complex situation. Instead of being rid of Donnelly and the FBI, he found himself stuck in a real life "tar baby"—Rick Donnelly. He would have to explain how he knew Donnelly. And, he knew he would have to stand by these boys, because Agent Frank Deal was going to be back in this office. Again.

FIFTY-TWO

By late that same afternoon, even as Michael, Zach, and Bubba were meeting with Drew Campbell, Rick Donnelly was driving through the outlying suburbs of Austin, Texas, looking for a rare piece of communication technology—a pay phone. Having escaped Tuscaloosa, Donnelly drove all night in his Ford Ranger along secondary highways and county roads. He kept awake with vast quantities of coffee, cold night air blowing in through open windows, and loud country music. Though sleep deprived and a little punchy, Rick looked forward to meeting up with Dave Knox and getting out of sight.

Rick finally found a working pay phone on the corner of a busy intersection in a convenience store parking lot. Someone had mounted the phone low enough so that the driver of a car didn't have to get out to make a call—a throwback to the days before cell phones! Rick paid his fifty cents and called Knox's cell. He picked up immediately.

"Hey Dave!" Rick said. "I'm in town."

"Oh man! That's great! We were getting worried about you, but I told them to chill out. Where are you now?" Dave asked, not masking his relief.

Rick consulted some street signs and gave Dave his location.

"Is there somewhere around there you can wait without any problem? I'll send a car for you right now, and I don't want to hear any complaints. You had your time off, now we have to get to work," Dave said.

Rick gave in. "Yeah, there's a Denny's across the street. I'll get something to eat and wait there. What should I do with my truck?"

"Just point it out to the people picking you up. They'll take care of it. You won't need it any more. I'll see you in about an hour. The Doyens want to meet you," Dave said.

"No problem. I'm a mess from driving all night, but I'm good to go."

"Yeah, now that you're here, we are good to go. In fact, you and I are going to take a big step toward making the entire plan good to go!"

Dan Klasing

FIFTY-THREE

After broadly describing the FBI's investigation of Donnelly, Drew asked whether Michael, Zach, and Bubba would agree to speak to the agent in charge. He didn't go into further detail or try to explain how the FBI suspected Donnelly of the theft of government secrets. However, he did explain that this surprising connection between Jimbo, his unknown associates, and Donnelly would be of immense interest to the FBI. All of the college students sitting in his office were understandably apprehensive, but Drew assured them that they had done nothing wrong, broken no laws, and would probably just be asked to spend a few hours explaining their experience to an agent.

Michael, Zach, and Bubba were all nineteen years old and legal adults. They could make their own decision about cooperating with the FBI. Campbell offered to call their parents and explain the situation or recommend counsel, but each of the frat brothers refused. They agreed to meet with an agent as long as Campbell could be in the room. He agreed. And then Drew did something he really, really didn't want to do. He called Agent Frank Deal.

Deal sat down in Campbell's conference room ten minutes later.

"What's this about?" Deal asked Campbell. "These boys have some information about our subject? Did you know anything about this before today?"

273

"Donnelly. Yes, they do. And no, I didn't. Michael's father," Drew gestured toward Michael, "called me this morning and asked if I would talk to his son and his friends about a little, well, adventure they had last night. It wasn't until they came here that I found out about any connection between their story and Donnelly. I've known Michael's father, Allen King, for many years. The rest is just coincidence."

"It may be coincidence. But I can't help noticing you seem to appear over and over in this investigation," Deal said.

"Yeah, I'm quite sure you did. I had no great desire to see you here in my conference room. But here you are! Lucky me," Campbell deadpanned back at Deal. "These gentlemen are all of age and have agreed to speak with you, at my request. They ask that I be allowed to remain, so I hope you don't have a problem with that."

"Fine. I hear you. We'll stop the thrust and parry and get to the point. Gentlemen," Deal said, faintly mimicking Drew, "why don't you just tell me what happened last night."

So, for the third time that day, Michael, with Bubba providing the color commentary, described Zach's interactions with Jimbo, the skinheads, the fire, and their having to avoid Jimbo and his associates later that night.

Deal listened carefully, rarely interrupting. He needed the entire picture first. After listening to the entire episode, Deal sat back in his chair thinking. *What possible connection could some fraternity boy have to a suspected murderer and traitor? And why were he and these other people after Donnelly? This just didn't make sense.*

"Are you sure you heard the name 'Donnelly'?" Deal asked Zach. "This is important, maybe more than you will ever realize, but I need to be sure."

"I'm sure Agent Deal, I really am. When Mr. Campbell said the name, I knew that was it. For sure," Zach answered.

The chances were just too remote that two people named Donnelly would be the subject of searches by two separate groups. *No, Deal thought, there's a connection between this Jimbo and Donnelly. Maybe the trail to Donnelly hadn't grown quite as cold as he feared.*

That connection might have become even stronger than the long odds of simultaneous manhunts if the FBI knew about the one fatality from the fire. But they didn't. It had been less than twenty-four hours and the body of Mikey's victim had yet to be discovered. The fire had consumed much of the hotel and reduced the kitchen, and the corpse within, to ashes. As it would turn out, he was only in the hotel to give an acquaintance a ride home and the hotel staff reported that all the guests and employees made it out of the building unharmed. Adding to the delay, nobody would ever even report the unidentified Latino as missing. Like most undocumented aliens, the few friends he had in the country kept their distance from the authorities.

"What are the chances that this Jimbo would tell the truth if I went to your frat house?" Deal asked all three boys.

Zach thought for a second and then responded. "I'd say zero. I think Jimbo was taking orders from someone. And I think he'd be more scared of the skinheads than of the FBI. Plus, his family is big in this state. Real big. I bet they have lawyers on call twenty-four/seven just to keep family members away from the cops, uh, FBI or whoever."

Michael added, "Yeah. Zach's right. We didn't see anyone do anything illegal, including Jimbo. Zach heard him talking to a bunch of rednecks, we saw those guys talking to people at the fire scene, and we all saw Jimbo talking to them again in the parking lot at the house. That's it. Yeah, Jimbo would just clam up, call his daddy, and then, well that's it. We've got no idea who the others guys were or where they came from."

"Jimbo's a real piece of work all right. You ain't going to find anything out. Hell, I bet we could find out more than you!" Bubba jokingly chided.

"Hmmmm," Deal said thinking about Bubba's comment. "You know what? I think you guys are right. We could pull this Jimbo in and put the screws on him. But we can't hold him on any charges. So if he decides to keep his mouth shut, we'll have showed our hand and the only lead we have dries up."

Michael now spoke up. "What if we tried? I mean, let the three of us try to find the connection from the

276

inside. We're around him all the time and Zach's his go-to guy in the house right now. Bubba used Zach once, there's a good chance he'd do it again. Jimbo likes to push people around."

"You mean us spy on him?" Zach asked quickly. "I don't think I want to be the bait."

"Aw, Zach, you don't get it," Bubba chimed in. "Jimbo's the bait. You're just the hook. Michael and I have your back. Don't worry about that. Anyway, Jimbo ain't much more than a puffed up bag of hot air anyway."

"Whoa, boys," Drew added. "You've done your job. Nobody's asking you to do anything like that. Leave it to these guys," he said, pointing at Deal. "They know what they're doing."

Deal listened to this exchange. Struck by what these three had accomplished, completely on their own, he carefully considered Michael's suggestion.

"That's not a bad idea at all. We have nothing else on Donnelly now. We absolutely have to follow this thread, but it's thin and we can't afford to break it." Deal said, thinking out loud. Then he looked up, a small smile crossing his face.

"You guys ever thought about going into undercover law enforcement?"

FIFTY-FOUR

Six Months Later

Dr. Rick Donnelly and Dr. Dave Knox worked through the winter in their private lab on the University of Texas campus. Comfortable apartments, set up right next to the lab, allowed them to remain totally concealed. They rarely saw the sun as they concentrated solely on re-creating and perfecting the manufacturing process to make Element 128 available in unlimited quantities. Once they had the process in hand, they used their respective engineering expertise to create the actual chemical processing equipment that would perform the production work.

With possession of this technical miracle, The Klass had unlimited and exclusive access to the only fuel known to man that could power a gravity wave reactor. The work they had done at Area 51 was, quite literally, brilliant. But Donnelly and Knox surpassed even that achievement with the efficiency of their production equipment. No larger than a standard refrigerator in its final configuration, their invention could take in raw materials and reconfigure the requisite molecular structures. Through precise manipulation of pressure and temperature, the atomic number of the resulting material could be raised to 128. Production capacity stood at "unlimited."

Donnelly and Knox's procurement of the production process from right under the government's nose and destruction of all backups set the Air Force, United States government, and Lockheed back at least five years. The Klass now held the singular and exclusive ability to power any number of gravity wave generators continuously. Meanwhile, the Air Force could only use its prototype GW-FB1 aircraft for less than five minutes. It took weeks to create enough Element 128 by hand production in a laboratory before it could fly again. In reality, nobody could, or would, be able to duplicate the now named Donnelly-Knox process for years to come.

The day after the first successful production run of Element 128, several of The Doyens visited the secret laboratory to witness the new equipment in action. Rick and Dave demonstrated the ease and simplicity of feeding various raw materials, none of which was exceedingly rare, into their machine. The operator would then simply tap a touch pad, causing a sophisticated computer program to take over the entire process. And after just a few minutes, Element 128 automatically dispensed into a shielded stainless steel container the size of a large test tube. One production cycle created enough fuel to power a gravity wave reactor, like the one on the GW-FB1 aircraft, continuously, for over a week.

Governors Smith and Burns, who Dave had met earlier in Atlanta, patiently watched the entire demonstration, along with the governor of Texas, Margie Franks. Dave Knox knew Franks well, but she had to be introduced to Rick Donnelly. Governor Franks impressed Rick with her pertinent questions and level of understanding of the complex science they had achieved in such a short time. Little did he know that Franks, just months earlier, had ordered his kidnapping. The question of whether he would have been forcefully brought to Austin or just killed outright became moot when he voluntarily joined in the effort to provide The Klass with the precious fuel.

The Doyens showed their pleasure at the success Dave and Rick achieved, congratulating them over and over. Governor Burns eventually hushed the small crowd.

"Gentlemen. You have achieved a scientific and technological breakthrough that will be remembered through the ages. But more importantly, you have gifted the South with a unique asset; one only we possess and which cannot be reproduced for many years to come. I say to you now, you stand in the same shoes as Benjamin Franklin, Thomas Payne, and Thomas Jefferson, the creative geniuses that were indispensible in freeing us from the oppression of an intolerable monarchy. Your reward will be the freedom the good people of the South shall enjoy from similar oppression. Plus of course, bountiful tangible reward, as promised."

Rick and Dave and tried not to beam with pride, but failed.

As The Doyens left the underground lab together, Governor Burns put his hand on Margie Franks' shoulder. Speaking into her ear, he said: "How does it feel Madam

President, to be one giant step closer to becoming the Mother of your country?"

Epilogue

Brookly Airfield sits at the Southern edge of Mobile, Alabama. The Airbus U.S. Manufacturing Facility, where the A320 family of jet airliners is assembled, occupies the northern end of the two-runway facility. Alabama successfully attracted the giant European aircraft manufacturer to the state with unequaled tax incentives and the promise of non-unionized labor.

In contrast to the giant gleaming white Airbus buildings, several dingy and much smaller hangars reside at the opposite end of runway 181. On a cool, rainy night in early spring, the doors on one of those hangars slid silently open and the pointed nose of an aircraft slowly appeared from within the darkened interior. Only a few dim lights guided the craft as it emerged into open air for the first time. The front of the craft seemed to grow wider and wider as it was drawn from within by a single tow vehicle. Finally, like an eaglet fighting its way out of its shell, the tips of the wings appeared. Looking from above, one could see two black eyes, like those of a manta ray, in the middle of the craft protruding ever so slightly above its black skin.

Once fully outside the building that had been its womb for the past year and a half, the entire craft seemed poised, ready and willing to launch itself into the sky for the first time.

The lone driver of the tow vehicle stopped after the craft cleared the hangar doors by only twenty feet. He unhooked from the front landing gear and disappeared back into the darkness of the hanger's interior. The hangar doors closed again, leaving the strange craft alone in the misting rain.

No lights appeared anywhere on its body, and it bore no markings of any kind. For a full minute, it remained perfectly still, nearly invisible in the gloom of the deep night.

Then, a small blue glow appeared from below each wing, and a rush of air exploded outward from beneath. Yet, after the momentary burst of wind, the craft fell silent. Without another sound of any kind, the craft rose straight up, its tricycle landing gear disappearing the moment it left the ground. It's upward movement stopped as it reached the height of the hangar's roof, momentarily suspended in the air as if taking a last look at its birthplace. Then, it disappeared, straight up into the night sky. If there had been someone directly beneath this newborn predator, they would have had only a second to see the huge black triangle before instantaneous acceleration carried it out of view.

More About Dan Klasing

Dan's love of history and his life in the South fuel his imagination. An avid fan of historical fiction, non-fiction biographies and political thrillers, Dan's characters confront situations inspired by current headlines and historical events. Over the past 25 years practicing law in Alabama, Dan has encountered a wealth of fascinating tales and unique personalities to draw upon. Dan lives with his wife Leslie and two daughters in Birmingham, Alabama.

Find out more at: **Facebook.com/TheKlassBooks/**

Acknowledgements

My thanks and love to Leslie, Anita and Katie for their patience and support while I wrote this book.

A special thanks to an outstanding author and friend, G. Allen Mercer, whose guidance and encouragement have been invaluable.

Look for the exciting follow up to The Klass with the second book in the series, *The Klass – Doyens!*

58473373R00161

Made in the USA
Charleston, SC
11 July 2016